The Billionaire's Prized Surrogate

He wants a baby, by any means necessary...

Claire's bored of her old routine as a history professor and wants to shake things up, so applies for a reality show, *Let's Make a Baby.* Harvey Grace, a handsome, single billionaire who yearns for a child, will pick a surrogate mother from five women. He selects Claire, and soon she's carrying a baby for him.

But they're both getting more than they bargained for - they're falling in love, and all in front of the reality show cameras. However, Harvey's unable to let himself fall too deep - women in the past have only been after his money. And when the show's producers bring on Claire's estranged sister Mercedes, she drives a wedge between the two lovebirds.

12/19

Will their new found love be torn apart beyond repair? Or can they find the strength to overcome all obstacles and become a loving family? Find out in this heartwarming clean romance by Shani Badu of BWWM Club.

Get Free Romance eBooks!

Hi there. As a special thank you for buying this book, for a limited time I want to send you some great ebooks completely **free of charge** directly to your email! You can get it by going to this page:

www.saucyromancebooks.com/physical

You can see a the cover of these books on the next page:

www.AfroRomanceBooks.com/RomanceBooks

www.AfroRomanceBooks.com/RomanceBooks

These ebooks are so exclusive you can't even buy them. When you download them I'll also send you updates when new books like this are available.

Again, that link is:

www.saucyromancebooks.com/physical

Contents

www.AfroRomanceBooks.com/RomanceBooks

More Books By Shani Badu - Page 384

Chapter 1

Waves of heat kept surging through Claire's body as she sat in her dressing room, waiting for a production assistant to come in and mic her. Sweat was leaking profusely from almost every crevice and pore on her body. Knots tightened in her stomach. She felt like she was going to throw up. She had never been this nervous in her entire life.

Just outside her door, a whole mass of people were gathering in the studio to witness the taping of what would soon become one of America's hottest TV shows. She could hear the hustle and bustle of staff getting everything ready and squared away before recording began. In merely a few minutes, she would be out on stage before a live audience of hundreds, as they watched her and four other women compete for the affection of a "lucky" bachelor. The sheer thought nearly made her keel over. Beside her on the counter was a pint of brandy, which she gladly helped herself to. She needed something to calm her nerves. Thankfully, one of the producers had equipped her room with a choice selection of alcohol, just in case Claire found herself getting cold feet.

There was no time for reneging, though. The executive producers made it abundantly clear to Claire that there was no turning back. She willingly signed her name on the dotted line when she applied for this gig. The contract was sealed, and there was nothing she could do about it. Besides, she already sacrificed her only means of living just to be here. Just three weeks prior, she resigned from her position as a history professor at Zender Community College to be a part of this show. The school's budget diminished drastically, so that meant major cutbacks on teachers' salaries. Instructors with shorter tenures unfortunately got the brunt of it, and Claire was among these.

Knowing for a fact that her reduced income would not support her lifestyle, she opted to look for other work. She searched high and low for a new job, subscribing to various employment sites for notifications about work opportunities. In the midst of checking her email one day, she came across a casting call looking for "surrogate mothers with engaging personalities for a juicy televised project." Claire immediately jumped on the opportunity, knowing full well that pregnancy couldn't be further from her reality. Casting directors emphasized that applicants for the show *must* be no more than two to three weeks pregnant to be considered, and *had* to take a valid pregnancy test. Claire was somehow able to pull one over on them by using an old pregnancy test from a friend who had recently had a baby. Production was so bent on getting the show up and running that they failed to do a background check to verify if that was indeed Claire's *actual* test. They really liked her personality, however, and thought she would be a great character for the show, so they quickly advanced her through all of the audition rounds. She did her final screen test to see how she would look on TV, and once that happened, she was cast for the show.

A week later, she got an email from producers detailing when filming would begin, how the format would go, the "role" they wanted her to play, and, of course, an attached contract that told her how much she would be compensated for her time. Because the show would be airing on a major cable network, they were willing to pay quite a bit for her participation. The basic premise of the show was a handsome, young bachelor has to choose from five women to be the surrogate mother of his baby, and he must subsequently spend nine months with the woman he selects. If Claire happened to be the lucky contender he chose, she would be paid a weekly stipend of $500. That meant over the course of the entire shooting, she could earn somewhere around

$18,000. Not to mention the residuals she would be getting every time the show aired. The only problem was, if she *was* chosen, there would be no baby to film growing inside of her. And that was a secret she preferred to keep hidden from the producers.

At any rate, she was here, about to put her life before hundreds—and later, millions—of people. Finally, a production assistant entered her dressing room, frantic as ever, scrambling to get a microphone attached to her body. The PA looked young and scared, probably an intern who had just started and was being thrust in every direction by the higher-ups.

"I need to find somewhere to hide the battery pack!" she cried nervously. She glanced at her watch and saw that time was ticking. Only about three minutes until filming officially began.

Claire tried to help her out by feeling around on her dress for some type of opening that would fit a small, black box inconspicuously. Then she had the bright idea to just throw a blazer on and put the battery pack in one of the pockets. Good thing she brought an extra piece of wardrobe, just in case.

"Ugh, thank you!" The PA made sure the box was totally concealed and then ran the wires through the inside of Claire's blazer so those wouldn't be seen either. She clipped the mic onto her lapel and practically pushed her out the door. "Okay, you're all set! They want you in your seat on stage!"

Claire felt like she was being thrown in a lion's den. The backstage area was dark and intimidating. She looked around her at the ropes descending from the rafters up top, the giant velvet curtains, and massive spotlights that shone even from behind the stage. She couldn't really see much of what was happening on the other side, just a sliver of the huge audience who was chattering away. She could see bright blue and purple lights swishing into each other from where she was standing. Classic jazz was loudly playing in the background. What sounded like an emcee was trying to entertain the audience until show time. They were making this a bit more theatrical than she expected.

"They need you out there! We don't have time for you to stand here and admire the place. Come on!" A pushy producer had found her and grabbed her by the arm, pulling her towards the stage. “Go sit next to Blondie, alright? That empty chair is all you,” he said, running back towards a control room.

Claire awkwardly staggered onto stage and looked out into the hundreds—what felt like billions—of indistinct faces staring at her. She was so nerve-racked that she couldn’t decipher how the crowd received her. Were they upset that she took so long to come out? Were they taken aback by her beauty? What was going through their minds? Claire instantly felt self-conscious. She then turned to the other four contestants who were glaring at her as if she had just committed a heinous crime. All of them looked like self-absorbed, snooty primadonnas. Claire landed her gaze on the blonde chick that the producer had told her to sit beside. She seemed to be the most “plastic” of all the contestants. Large boobs, at least a G-cup, Claire joked in her head, absurdly long, blonde hair extensions, pink, puckered lips that only evidenced overindulgence in collagen injections. Just a manufactured mess. And Claire had to sit next to this train wreck.

"Do we have our fifth and final babe?" the host blurted out. Claire hadn't even noticed this guy, but he was standing off to the opposite end of the stage. Tall, lanky, and dark with salt-and-pepper hair. He had the stature of a basketball player, a well-seasoned, retired one. He had to at least be in his early to mid-fifties. Regardless, Claire thought he was kind of cute. She had secretly wished that *he* was the suitor.

The other four ladies giggled pretentiously, sounding just like catty high school girls. Claire rolled her eyes, realizing that she was dealing with a bunch of fake actresses instead of real women. Was what he said really that funny, she thought. She took a moment to absorb the extravagant set. Lots of pastels—pinks, purples, yellows, and blues. Rich carpet, gigantic monitors, an enormous sign that read 'Let's Make a Baby.' The budget for this show must have been steep, because everything was so glamorous and gleaming, almost taking a cue from 'The Price Is Right.' She looked over at the timer just above the audience and saw that there was only thirty seconds until the show started.

Claire couldn't believe she was here. She never thought in a million light-years that she would be cast for a reality TV show. But there was this nagging feeling of guilt that kept churning around in her stomach. Her hands grew clammy as she worried if somewhere down the line, she would be exposed. She wasn't naïve to the tricks that producers liked to play on these shows. She had heard horror stories of people having their dirt surface at the most inopportune times. But it wasn't just fear of being found out that put her on edge. The mere fact that she was going to be on television was heart-pounding enough. She didn't want to embarrass herself by stuttering when she spoke, or do something weird that the cameras caught. What if she was rejected by the suitor? Could she handle being rejected in front of millions of viewers? All these thoughts were swirling in her mind, as a production assistant stood at the foot of the stage to count down the last five seconds before recording started.

"All clear," a voice said over a speaker. The tall host took his position on the 'x' at the center of the stage that the audience couldn't see. The PA pointed, signaling that cameras were rolling. Cheesy, traditional game show music sounded over the audio system. The blue and purple lights danced all over the place, blinding Claire every time they flashed her way. She felt queasy and lightheaded. A camera attached to the end of a long, mechanical arm descended from out of nowhere and drew in close to the host.

"Good evening, everyone, welcome to the premiere of 'Let's Make a Baby!' I'm your host, Antoine Cabrera, and we've got a very intriguing show for you guys tonight! A charming, attractive suitor will be choosing from among these lovely ladies to my left to carry his baby."

A sign that read 'Audience' lit up in a corner adjacent to the stage, prompting the hundreds of spectators in the stands to say "ooooh" for dramatic effect. So contrived, Claire thought. But that was "reality TV" for you.

"We have a young, wealthy bachelor on today's episode who's going to take each of our five ladies out on a date, just to see which one of them will be the perfect match to mother his child. But we'll get to meet him a little bit later. First, let's introduce our gorgeous tenderonis," Antoine said with a wink. "On the far right, we have the beautiful Tiara Turner, a classy Southern Belle hailing from Alabama."

Tiara cheesed and gave the stereotypical pageant queen wave. She looked adorable though, with her milk chocolate skin, snow white teeth, and huge brown eyes. She was wearing a very sparkly silver dress with jet black stripes cutting through the waist.

“Miss Tiara, please tell us about yourself,” Antoine said, pacing around the middle of the stage.

“Okay, well, I’m 23 years old, I’m a registered nurse, I consider myself to be very romantic, I love long walks on the beach, and my ideal guy is someone with a lot of money and great hair.” The audience laughed. She almost had the voice and attitude of a Valley Girl, except her inflection was annoyingly high-pitched. She sounded nothing like someone from the South. Claire’s stomach turned once she realized that she would have to introduce herself. She wasn’t ready for that at all. None of the producers told her that she would have to do that. She was told that the host himself would introduce all the contenders, and all they had to do was sit there and look pretty.

“Alrighty, thank you, Tiara. I’m sure the bachelor we have backstage will be to your liking,” Antoine teased. “Next, we have the stunning Clarissa Kingston, a feisty go-getter representing Jersey!”

Clarissa stood up and did a twirl, showing off all her assets. Claire rolled her eyes, thinking that this chick was being absolutely extra for camera time. She clearly wanted to stand out and make herself known. There was no question about that, for she was donning a loud, hot pink club dress that barely came down past her thighs. Huge, golden hoop earrings, black extensions with purple highlights, and a ridiculously large bow that sat to the side of her head.

"Clarissa, give us some words," Antoine demanded.

"Sure, Antoine. I'm 25 years old, I *used* to be an exotic dancer, I think that I can really make a man feel good, I love doing fun and crazy things like skydiving, and my ideal guy is someone who's not afraid to embrace his sexuality. Like if he has a kinky fetish, I'm all for it." The audience whirled and whooped at what she said.

"Whoa! Whoa!" Antoine said, as the audience continued hollering at her brash statement. "You're not wasting any time letting us know what's up, huh?" He smiled, shaking his head in disbelief. "That's okay, though. I've seen and heard way worse." He chuckled, and so did the audience.

Claire was not for any of the antics that were happening right now. Everything just seemed so artificial. From the corny jokes to the presentation. It just wasn't sitting well with her. Not to mention the misinformation from production. She was only two people away from having to open her mouth and briefly say something about herself, and it had to be witty, interesting, or funny. What could she possibly come up with on the spot? Claire was not a think-on-your-toes kind of person. She had a certain wit about her, but sucked at making up stuff on the fly. That just wasn't her forte.

As the third girl introduced herself, Claire tuned out of reality for a moment, racking her brain for words to say. To avoid drawing attention to herself, she put herself on autopilot, pretending as if she was all engaged in the action when really, she was stuck inside her head until she could find a clever intro. Next thing she knew, it was the fourth girl's turn. Claire's stomach bubbled and whined. The queasiness returned. She thought it was just a temporary feeling of nausea, but it was staying. And it was getting worse. It felt like her guts would erupt from her gullet at any second. She kept swallowing to suppress the urge to vomit. Her face grew very hot and her ears felt like they instantly became flooded. As the fourth girl got up and pranced around on stage, clearly trying to one-up the ex-stripper chick, Claire felt like she was falling forward. Her diaphragm heaved involuntarily, and before she knew it, she spewed chunks all over the stage.

*****

“Claire, are you okay?” a production assistant asked, attaching a mic to Claire’s lapel. “You’ve been out for like the past couple hours.”

Claire, disoriented and groggy, sat up on the couch holding her head. Once she realized where she was, a gush of relief washed over her. That whole fiasco she thought she was a part of was only a dream—more like a nightmare. “I’ve been sleep for that long?”

“Yeah. We thought we were gonna have to postpone filming, because we didn’t think you’d wake up in time.” The PA laughed.

“Geez. I didn’t know I checked out like that.” She stared off, embarrassed. “Sometimes when I’m *really* nervous about something, I get really sleepy. I guess that’s a defense mechanism my body has against anxiety. To just shut itself down.”

“You’re fine, you don’t have to explain yourself. As long as we can shoot these scenes before night falls. Harvey and the other ladies are waiting for you at the hotel. We’ve gotta get you there ASAP." She helped Claire up off the couch and led her outside to the production car, a 2015 black Escalade. "When you get there, there should be a bald guy at the front entrance. He'll be wearing a red vest with the network logo on it. That's Rodney. He's one of the executive producers, and he'll take you where you need to go, okay? The cameras will start filming as soon as you step out the car. Try not to look at them, just act naturally, be yourself and relax. You obviously had enough personality to get cast, so don't feel like you have to put on for the cameras, okay? You're gonna do fine."

Claire nodded apprehensively. She had no idea what to expect when she arrived. For all she knew, she could be set up by producers to get ambushed by the other ladies—verbally or otherwise. Her heart pounded as a million predictions ran through her mind. Then she started wondering how she would look on TV. Now she would be cognizant of which angle the camera caught her at, because she did not want to be caught in an unflattering shot. But then she can't look at the camera to know where it was. So how could she be fully aware of its position at all times? She couldn't. And it was time for her to face that reality.

*****

Claire took a deep, shaky breath before she was beckoned by a producer to come from around the corner of the hotel. She tried her hardest to maintain a natural composure, but all she could think about was if she was walking funny or if her makeup or clothes looked awkward on tape. How did the people calling the shots expect you to look and behave normally when there were all these extra factors to think about? At any rate, this was just a walk-up scene, and if need be, they would re-shoot—and re-shoot and re-shoot until she got it right. Who could've known that so much went behind filming a simple, less-than-ten-second walking scene? She managed to pull it off though. A producer yelled, "Let's cut it, guys!"

He went up to Claire and gave her direction for the next bit. "Okay, so that's out the way. Now we're going to bring Harvey out, and we're gonna get a shot of you seeing him for the first time. So give us your best, most authentic reaction, alright? Then we'll have him introduce himself to you, offer to have dinner with you, you two sit at the table and eat, he's gonna get to know you, blah, blah, blah. After that, he's going to announce his decision on the rooftop. It'll be the dramatic conclusion to the first episode!" The producer was excited about the big finish. As if this type of format was so original and had never been done before. A unique take on the format, but still nothing new. “And just so you know, he’s already filmed his scenes with the other ladies, so you’re the best for last, sweetheart.”

He ran back behind the camera and gestured for a PA to get Harvey out there. Claire stood in angst, as she watched with anticipation for him to come out. *What would he look like*, she thought. Would he be tall and muscular, short and stocky, average and slender? These thoughts circled her head, not because she was superficial and was concerned only about how attractive this man would be, but she wondered how his looks would mesh with hers. Certain physical appearances don’t work for television and producers always take that into account when casting people. Hopefully, whoever this Harvey guy was wouldn’t look weird with Claire. She was tall and slim, about 5’9” with smooth, dark chocolate skin and short black hair that gave off African queen vibes. A pretty distinguishable woman to stand next to. Not just anybody could fit right with her.

A gentleman proceeded out the French doors that led into the posh bistro which sat on the side of the hotel. He was slightly taller than Claire but had a husky upper build. It was apparent that he worked out. He had blonde hair that was slicked back and edged up on the sides. He also had striking, icy blue eyes that penetrated through his thick, black spectacles. Very sharp square jaw that throbbed as he clenched his teeth. The aura Claire got from him was bona fide Clark Kent of the Daily Planet, except this guy was way more debonair. At the first sight of him, her eyes widened and her mouth gaped open before it slowly formed a pleased smile. She liked what she saw. He approached her in a suave manner, taking her hand in his and kissing it. Chivalry—kind of what she was expecting from him. She was smitten by him right now. But then her mind immediately shifted back to the "reality" of reality TV and wondered if he was being this way to look good on camera. He gazed into her eyes though, and it was the most sincere look any man had ever given her which had her questioning her own skepticism.

"Nice to meet you, gorgeous. I'm Harvey." There was something a bit quirky about him that she couldn't put her finger on, but it would reveal itself if she got the chance to film with him for nine months.

"Hi," Claire replied, like a shy schoolgirl. "I-I'm Claire."

“Allow me to take you to dinner so we can get to know each other a little better,” he proposed.

Chapter 2

Claire's chest was fluttering a thousand miles a minute. She felt her stomach nearly come up through her throat. Nausea overcame her at once. *Oh no*, she thought. *Please don't let me throw up all over the place like in my dream. Please don't tell me that nightmare was a foreshadow of what was to come*. Just like in her dream, she kept swallowing her saliva, hoping that she could push down whatever wanted to come up. A production assistant looked at her funny and started to come over and see what the problem was, but he hesitated. The last thing he wanted was a public lashing for ruining a scene that was in the process of taping. The supervising producer, Stan, was all into the moment, totally oblivious to what was going on other than what was happening directly in front of the cameras.

Harvey stood before the five women, holding a glass of champagne in one hand and a mysterious box in the other. It was small and velvety. Hopefully not an engagement ring. Claire's heart palpitated like crazy when she thought of the possibility that this guy might just propose marriage. Of course production would throw a monkey wrench into the mix.

Harvey teasingly fumbled the box around in his hand. Claire found herself completely fixated on it, as she juggled with theories of what could be in there. The camera guy focused right on Harvey, panning from his face to his hand for a dramatic shot.

"Alright, Harvey. I want you to start your little preface speech now," Stan directed. "Remember to talk slowly, *do not* rush to reveal your final decision. We wanna build up as much tension as possible. Tease us a little. Make us think you're going to pick one person when you're really not. You know what to do, kid. You've seen these kinda shows before." Stan stepped off to the side to light up a cigarette. "If we can do this in one, clean take, that'd be lovely."

Harvey took a breath before he started. The cameras were still rolling. "Okay, ladies," he began, looking at all five of them in the eye. "It's been such a pleasure getting to know all of you. I think each one of you has something unique and different to bring to the table, and I like that. I like that you all are your own person with a distinct flavor." He flashed a half smile that would make even the strongest-minded woman swoon. "I could honestly see myself with every single one of you, but unfortunately, I can only choose one." He paused for effect.

"Good, Harvey! That's the kinda fluffy crescendo we're looking for! You're off to a good start, bud! Keep on this road," Stan shouted from behind the main camera. Harvey turned to look at him, irritated. Then he turned his attention back to the women.

"After taking you all out on dates, and getting to know you, I came to appreciate each of your stunning qualities. Amber, our time together was amazing." He faced a petite brunette who had to have been no more than twenty-one or twenty-two, a baby.

"I'm glad we were able to venture around the city and share our personal stories with one another. I think there was a very… interesting dynamic between us. For us to have such a lighthearted physical experience, but still be comfortable enough to divulge our deep, dark past…there's undeniable chemistry there. Amber, I can definitely see you as the mother of my child. You're genuine and real and transparent. Surely, the baby will inherit those wonderful traits."

Claire was really listening to what Harvey was saying, and *how* he was saying it. The way he came off now was much different than how he presented himself when she was on a date with him. Just an hour ago at dinner, the entire conversation they had was about him. Initially, there was a fair exchange between them, but then as Harvey grew more comfortable, he started rambling all about himself. His aspirations, his likes and dislikes, the places he's been, the women he's dated. Claire couldn't get a word in edgewise. But here, he seemed to be much more considerate. Producers probably told him to be like that for this particular scene, although he did sound somewhat genuine with what he was saying, so maybe not. Claire couldn't help but wonder how they would edit his persona on TV, though. Would viewers get the self-absorbed version or the thoughtful version, the one with depth and sincerity? Then she wondered how they would edit *her*. Thus far, she hadn't really given them much to work with. She tried to be as even-tempered and diplomatic as possible without ruffling too many feathers. She didn't think that was going over well with the producers, because to them, those are ingredients for a bland character.

As it stood now, she was not living up to her claim of having an "engaging personality" like the casting call asked for. But it was pretty much understood what they meant by "engaging personality." They wanted someone who was polarizing or controversial, someone with a large ego, or someone who was hotheaded and volatile. *That* makes good television. Someone with an intriguing story was secondary. But Claire's nerves—and her resolve to be herself no matter what—got in the way of any of that. She was not about to intensify her personality for an edited TV show. During preliminary interviews, producers asked her a series of questions after showing her unbecoming footage of the other ladies. They wanted her, of course, to talk trash about them after she witnessed how disgusting or sloppy they were. And, in typical reality TV fashion, to amp up the drama, there was no question that they would show her interview to the other ladies to stir the pot. Claire would not give them the satisfaction, though. She had the fire in her, but opted to tread lightly, especially since she didn't know any of these women from Adam.

Harvey moved on to talking about the next girl. A sultry black beauty named Kat. The camera panned from Amber to her, as she stood a little more erect and plastered this semi-fake smile on her face. She was very pretty though, probably the prettiest amongst the five. Long black hair curled at the ends, big, shiny white teeth, full luscious lips and a perfectly curved body. Her breasts and butt were just big enough to get a guy's attention, but not overly massive to where it looked like she had work done. She had the figure of someone who *should* be on TV.

"Kat, the word gorgeous doesn't even do you justice," Harvey flattered. Kat blushed. "I loved sitting VIP with you at the horse race in Verona Heights. Just from our dialogue, I can tell that you're a sophisticated, cultured woman who appreciates the finer side of life. You carry yourself with such class, and you have this unapologetic beauty. I know you'd be the type of mom who would only want the best for her child and would do everything in her power to make sure those nine months count."

Claire rolled her eyes and felt like she was going to throw up from the amount of sap that oozed out of Harvey's mouth. She doubted that all this rhetoric he was dishing out would even make the final cut when they packaged these episodes. Too much substance, not enough outrageous talk.

The next lady in line was similar in temperament to Claire. Very poised, mature, and aware of self, but with a silent edginess. Her name was Rhoda, and she had the same physique as Claire, except she was a bit taller and unequivocally European in features. Sharp, narrow nose, gaunt face, stark blue eyes, and long brown hair with olive skin. Her likeness was a mash-up of Iberian Peninsula, Scandinavian, and Mediterranean, her comportment being that of an elegant French woman. Stunning lady, definitely supermodel material. She was probably the best dressed out of all the contenders, wearing a red designer gown with brilliant sequins along the hem. Whether she dressed herself or had a stylist help her, getting a red dress was the smartest move to make. It's one of the most attractive colors on a woman.

"Rhoda, dear sweet Rhoda," Harvey started, looking off to the side as he swirled around his drink. The camera guy pulled back, probably for a full body shot of her magnificent garment. It was certainly worthy of exclusive attention. Harvey chuckled before he continued. "Your accent …your accent is sexy. You have this exotic look about you that I'm sure has turned many of heads. I'm not gonna lie, there was…a bit of a language barrier between us while we tried to communicate. But when we locked eyes, I knew we were on the same page —" Harvey was cut off by Claire glibly choking out of nowhere.

If that's not the corniest thing I've ever heard, Claire thought. The camera immediately turned to focus on her. She gawked at the lens like a deer stuck in headlights. Everyone, producers and all, looked at her. Inwardly, she shrank to the size of an infant. She just knew she had ruined the whole scene and they would have to do it all over again.

"I'm sorry. I didn't mean to choke like that. Can you guys just edit that out?" She looked pleadingly at the producers. There was thick silence for a moment, as everybody's eyes stayed glued to Claire. It was so quiet, you could hear a pin drop. The faint mechanical hum from the cameras couldn't even be heard. Stan stepped forward exhaling a large cloud of nicotine. He looked at Claire as if he wanted to yank her up and throw her against the glass doors behind her. But then he released a calm sigh and his expression softened a little. Claire didn't know how to read that.

"Relax, honey. That was actually TV gold," he said, surprising and relieving Claire at the same time. "Well not gold per se, but it's a nugget of entertainment goodness, let's say that." Stan was a bit eccentric in his gesticulations and that was becoming increasingly apparent to Claire as he talked.

"There needs to be some kinda resistance amongst the cast. Everything can't be hunky-dory. Ladies, take a cue from Miss Rexall, here. Let's rub our palms together and make a little more friction. You guys don't have to pull each other's hair out, but—okay, I don't wanna outright tell you girls to argue or get gully for the sake of interesting TV, but—you all know what to do," he said, getting somewhat frustrated with the women. But then it seemed as if he was frustrated with himself for not telling them this a lot earlier. "Stop being super classy and prudish. Bring out those claws a little. Don't attack each other, but get sassy with one another. Don't be afraid to speak your mind and step on some toes. Now come on, let's amp this up, people. I got too much dead footage here." He quickly turned to Harvey to assure him that he wasn't speaking of him in particular as the reason for this. Then he went over to Claire and whispered in her ear.

"Sweetheart, I don't usually do this, but I'm telling you upfront that your little sarcastic cough *will* more than likely end up in the edited episode. We need that. There's absolutely no opposition or anything. These ladies are boring. This is gonna be the first episode, the make-or-break debut, and only footage we have is of these girls standing around like mannequins. Who wants to watch that?" Claire sniggered as he pulled back and gave her a doubtful look. The whole production crew was on its toes, praying that this first day of filming go off without a hitch. Thus far, things weren't ideal, but Harvey's flattery and the ladies' dresses were the only things redeeming this otherwise lackluster taping.

Harvey looked around at the production assistants and producers for his cue to continue with his speeches. Claire's sudden choking spell seemed to disrupt the flow a little. Thus, everyone behind the scenes was scrambling to reassemble themselves, although the cameras were still rolling and mics were still recording. Stan returned to his place behind the camera. He looked and acted more like a director for a scripted feature film than an "impromptu" reality show. That's one of the things that made him quite peculiar. Unless he just saw himself as the Steven Spielberg of reality television. He pointed at Harvey, indicating that he wanted him to speak.

"Wait!" Stan shouted, walking back over to where the action was taking place. "Harvey, before you pick up where you left off with Rhoda, I need you to give me a surprised face or something, like you're still reacting to Claire's cough. We got a bit sidetracked, and I just want another reaction shot from you from a different angle so we can cut the two scenes together, alright? We can make this a tense slash comedic moment." He ran back over to his overseer spot.

Stan was a unique producer in that he was very forward about what he wanted to come across on screen. He was not shy in letting others know that even though this was "reality TV," it's still a production nonetheless and should therefore be treated as such. Of course, he kept in mind the golden rule that all producers must follow in this genre, which is to never tell the cast exactly what to do. He still didn't allow that to keep him from being as transparent as possible regarding his "vision" for the show. "Okay, let's wrap this up, guys! It'll be midnight before we finish this stupid scene!" Stan bent down and peered into the main camera's viewfinder. Harvey nodded in concurrence with his instruction from Stan.

The camera guy swiftly sidestepped over to face Harvey from a different direction. Harvey looked at Claire and forced his face into a flustered expression. He tried to make it look as unforced as possible.

"You alright over there?" he asked wryly.

"I'm fine, baby," Claire came back with some sass.

"Alright, just checking, dear. I was almost about to offer you a sip of my champagne to wash away whatever was stuck in your esophagus," Harvey retorted. "But I forgot you're pregnant. You can't drink alcohol." A knot instantly formed in Claire's throat. She knew the truth about that.

"Good!" Stan shouted. This was the kind of saucy exchange he was asking for, and the fact that it was between the suitor and the contender made it juicier!

Some of the other ladies giggled. Harvey mouthed something to Amber which made her laugh loud enough for the camera guy to focus on her. "Anyway," Harvey said, getting back to the business at hand. "As I was saying, Rhoda, despite the fact that you spoke little English, I still felt a genuine connection with you. Just sitting atop the Giordano Tower and looking over at the Montague Pier while we drank Moet was an enchanting experience. You carry yourself like a queen, a goddess. And hearing you talk in that beautiful Romanian accent was divine. Rhoda, what's your ethnicity? You told me where you're from, but I must know what flavor you are."

"Vwat flavor I am? My ethnee-city? Vwell, I am Portuguese, Italian, Spah-nish, und Lebanese," she answered.

"Ahh, that makes a lot of sense," Harvey replied. "You have very strong Latin roots mixed with a little Middle Eastern. I knew you were exotic."

"Yis. My great-grandmother was from Lebanon," she said proudly.

"That's beautiful." Harvey took a sip of champagne. "If only *I* could've impregnated you, I know our baby would be gorgeous. Not saying the one that's growing inside of you now won't be, darling, but I'm just saying. I'm a mixed breed myself. German, Finnish, and Venezuelan."

"Ahhh," Rhoda said astounded.

"Yeah." Harvey then turned his attention to the fourth contender, an average height blonde who was thick in all the right places. She was dripping Americana pride, sporting an acid-washed, flag-inspired cocktail dress. She had on sparkly, red pumps and blue, star-shaped earrings. Probably the least tasteful dresser amongst the women, but at least she showed her unabashed patriotism. Her demeanor was that of a

Southern conservative, which rubbed Claire the wrong way for obvious reasons.

"Emma, I just love your spunk and your heart. You have absolutely no shame and that's what endears me towards you." Harvey and Emma both laughed. "I like a woman who's not afraid to tell it like it is and refuses to cut corners. And those are the type of qualities I want my kid to have, be it a boy or girl. Emma, you're a fun time. We had a ball at the amusement park earlier today, and I could ride coasters with you for an eternity. You're definitely one of the liveliest people I've ever met." Emma blushed and looked at the ground shyly. Claire glanced at her out the corner of her eye, wondering how "lively" could even come close to describing this girl. She was a dud just like the rest, if not the worst. Even now, she didn't look like she would say or do anything interesting any time soon.

Harvey sighed and did something he hadn't done for the rest of the ladies. He walked over to Claire and stood directly in front of her. Stan looked baffled, as were the rest of the cast and crew. They weren't expecting him to do that. In fact, he wasn't supposed to do that. He was told that he could say whatever he wanted, as long as he stood in a single spot and delivered his speeches from there only.

Claire was just as confused as everyone else. Her eyes locked onto his, as if they were demanding an explanation.

"Claire. Um...wow. I'm actually speechless right now," he said, looking back at Stan. "Um. You're very different. There's something about you that I've never seen in a woman before. You're very, very intelligent, funny, adventurous, candid...you have this elusive quality about you that's really attractive. Makes me wanna get to know you more. You ever met someone that was so enigmatic that it literally pulled you to them? That's what I get from you."

Harvey took a deep breath and set his glass of champagne down on the ground. The camera intently followed his every move. He extended the small, velvety box towards Claire and dramatically opened it. Claire's heart raced as she tried to guess in her mind what it was before he revealed it to her. What she expected to be a ring was actually a bedazzled pacifier. Her mouth fell open in relief and shock.

"Claire Rexall...let's make a baby."

*****

Harvey was getting powdered up by a makeup artist in Claire's guest bedroom, which she was forced to turn into a makeshift dressing room. Harvey seemed to be basking in his fluffing session, turning his head this way and that, as if he was getting prepped to film a Hollywood scene. "Make sure you accentuate my sexy features, Brenda," he said raising his chin pompously while she dusted around his neck.

"What a narcissist," Claire mumbled under her breath. She took a swig of coffee waiting patiently for Harvey to film his little interview with Stan. Production had transformed one of her walk-in closets into a confessional. They draped a green screen against the wall, ran wires all throughout the place, set up hidden cameras and lights, the whole shebang. This would be where Stan would ask Harvey and Claire a series of incriminating questions, and where they could voluntarily vent their feelings to the viewers.

It had been about a week or so since Claire and Harvey last filmed together at the hotel rooftop. They were instructed not to contact one another for any reason until they were reunited to tape the pregnancy journey. And they obliged. But

Claire had quickly forgotten just how egotistical Harvey was, and seeing him in this light was perturbing to her. She had wondered, though, how someone so full of himself could have the heart to want and look after a child.

Stan came out from the confessional and requested Harvey's presence. Harvey flew into the walk-in closet. He was ready to be in front of those cameras. Stan wasted no time jumping right into the interrogation. He pushed the record button on the camera.

"Harvey, explain why you decided to use this show as a way to get a baby. Why couldn't you just go out, find a wife, and get her pregnant like every other normal person?"

"I'm not a normal guy. I didn't want to conform to traditional family roles because frankly, that's boring, and we live in the twenty-first century, who still does that? I feel like people should look for more inventive ways to do ordinary crap. I think having a child unconventionally is the way of the future."

Chapter 3

Claire felt so out of place being followed by a camera crew in Beverly Hills. It was unnerving and tense, especially with the nagging insecurity about how she looked on film. Not to mention, the thirsty Joe Schmoes that kept trying to interact with her just for camera time, not even knowing what was taking place to begin with. Every few steps, here came another one, looking for their fifteen minutes of fame. Production was constantly shooing them away like flies. If this was what it felt like to be a celebrity, she was totally fine with going back to a content nobody when this was all over. She had been taping for six weeks with Harvey, and one would think that she'd be used to this by now. But Claire didn't believe she'd ever fully adjust to it. It just wasn't in her nature to be in the limelight.

She and Harvey strolled down Rodeo Drive looking for a chic new maternity shop that just opened about a week ago. Harvey offered to update her wardrobe to accommodate her soon-to-be voluminous belly, one that would never come about. Fortunately, at this stage in the game, she was able to get away with not showing. But she still felt a smidgeon of guilt, having to play the part and just go with this for the sake of the show. However, she knew she wouldn't be able to keep up the lie for much longer. During these filming sessions, she had to be mentally present for the scene at hand, while simultaneously thinking of ways to make her charade stretch. The most obvious solution was to do like every other woman trying to fake a pregnancy and just stuff a pillow in her shirt or get one of those artificial pregnant tummies. But what would she do when they filmed her getting an ultrasound? That scene was inevitable. And how would she wiggle her way out of the climactic episode where she would finally have to go into labor and give birth to a *real* baby? Those were questions that needed answers, but for now, Claire put those concerns in the backburner of her mind and forced herself to pretend like they weren't problems. For now, she was going to play her role and go maternity shopping with Harvey.

They finally reached the store, Joveni. It was a nice little cutesy and quaint place with varying shades of pink and blue splashed everywhere. Lots of clashing patterns though, with the diagonal stripes, polka dots, and cross hatches running into each other on the walls. The faint aroma of bubblegum and freshly baked cookies kind of steered you away from the visually jarring nature of the wallpaper though. On the far back wall was the word 'Joveni' in huge padded form. The floors were covered with soft, cushiony, salmon pink carpet. Overall, there was a gentle, inviting energy that made you want to stay.

A red-haired, middle-aged woman, presumably the owner, came out from the back of the store to greet everyone. She excitedly grinned from ear to ear once she saw the cameras and boom poles, quickening her step to meet the cast and crew. Before she could even get within ten feet of the person closest to her, she extended her hand for a shake. The first person she made contact with was Stan, who had been anxious and fidgety the whole morning. He was on edge because prior to his scouting Joveni for filming, he had been rejected from at least four other locations that he intended to shoot at today. Now he was racking his brain for alternatives and that just made him a scattered mess. Filming at one place for the entire day wouldn't cut it.

He grabbed the woman's hand penitently. "Hi, Erma. It's nice to meet you. You have to forgive me if I seem a little… off, but I had an ordeal just trying to find a place to tape. Luckily, Harvey here was okay with doing a little maternity shopping for Claire." Claire and Harvey waved coyly at Erma.

She reciprocated. “I’m so grateful that you just opened this place literally last week. This is a Godsend.”

“Oh, you’re more than welcome, Stan. I’m actually quite thrilled that you would even consider filming in my little humdrum store, albeit by default. But I’m privileged nonetheless. Oh, and congratulations are certainly in order for the madam,” Erma said, looking cheerily at Claire. “It’s my pleasure to meet yet another expecting mother.” There was a mesmeric formal way about Erma that you didn’t typically find in people, something about her that made you listen to everything she said even if it did seem boring or old-fashioned.

“Nonsense, Erma. This store is far from ‘humdrum,’ dear. It’s quite eye-catching which is why I’m glad I chose to come here. Only qualm about this place is all the lines and dots and stuff everywhere. That might not translate favorably on TV, know what I mean?”

She nodded her understanding. “I getcha. Well, there are certain areas in the store that aren’t as cacophonous that you could possibly record at. This is a relatively large space, so I’m sure we could find something that’s compatible for television." She led Stan to a corner of the store with camera and sound guys in tow, leaving Claire and Harvey to stand back by themselves.

"Hey, could we just get a quick shot of this awesome Joveni sign in the back of the store?" Stan asked.

"Of course. Wherever you'd like to film, don't hesitate to ask," she said with a large smile. Erma was definitely happy about having a TV show filmed in her store. From the looks of it, this was probably the height of anything she'd ever done.

The crew shuffled over to the back, as Stan directed the camera guy on where to aim. Claire and Harvey waited patiently for them to get all their necessary B-roll footage.

"Hey, aren't they supposed to get all these extra little shots *after* they film the main attraction, *us*?" Harvey inquired to Claire. "I mean, I'm not an expert on this stuff by any means, but one thing I know is that should come last."

"You're asking the wrong person, pal. Beats me," Claire replied bluntly. "I was just told to show up to filming and that's it. I'm not privy to all this behind-the-scenes stuff."

Harvey chuckled. “Well, this isn’t the first reality show I’ve done, so I know how these things go.”

“But wait, I thought you said you weren’t an expert on this kinda stuff.” Claire side-eyed him. “But now, you’re saying this isn’t your first time at the rodeo?”

“Claire, just because I have *one* other reality show on my resume doesn’t make me an expert. I was just sayin’, I’m still not fully hip to how they run things. Besides, no two reality show productions are the same, trust me. I’ve heard stories,” Harvey explained. An awkward silence followed. “Hey, have you ever seen that show Billion-Heirs, about these teens who inherit crap loads of money from their relatives? It used to come on GypTV years ago.”

“Nope, never heard of it. I was never much of a TV watcher. I take it you’ve seen it though?”

“I did more than watch it. I was actually *on* it. They changed my name and everything for legal reasons. I was Peter on there. To this day, I still cringe at that name.” Harvey shivered jokingly, making Claire laugh. “That was like thirteen years ago though. I was seventeen.”

"I never would've guessed. So if you don't mind me asking, who did you inherit money from?"

"My parents," he replied somberly.

Claire went silent as if to pay respect to their memory. "What happened to them?" she mustered the courage to ask.

"They were robbed and murdered on their way to an opera. Killer was never caught." Harvey sniffed trying to suppress tears.

Claire gasped and covered her mouth. "I'm so sorry," she told him, her voice barely above a whisper.

"Nah, it's okay. My parents lived a nice, full life. They made sure that if anything happened to them, that I'd be taken care of. They had *billions* of dollars from insurance policies, international bank accounts, estates…in their will, they explicitly stated that they wanted me to have it all. I didn't have to divide it with anyone. Being an only child has its perks." He tried to push himself to at least smile at the fact that he was the sole heir of his parents' fortune. But the sadness of it all lingered all over his face.

"I'm sure your parents would be proud of you that you're doing well for yourself and you're eager to give them a grandchild." Claire attempted to steer the conversation towards optimism.

"Even though they'll never be able to see it?" Harvey asked sarcastically.

"You don't know that, though. When the baby's born, they might be looking down from wherever they are and see the little precious bundle of joy, and they'll smile that their son is trying to continue the Grace legacy."

A smirk slowly started to crack on Harvey's face. "You're right, Claire." He bent down to talk to her stomach. "Because my little baby is gonna be a radiant ball of cuteness when he or she comes out." He playfully tickled her belly, sincerely thinking something was forming in there. Claire couldn't help but feel like utter crap.

"Yeah, he or she is on their way," she said sheepishly.

"I can't wait 'til they get here," he said, rubbing circles on Claire's belly. She noticed how longingly he stared at her stomach, and sensed that it was the sincerest he'd ever been.

"Can I be honest with you?" Claire asked.

Harvey gradually rose up. "Sure," he said guardedly.

"When I first met you, I honestly didn't think you genuinely wanted a child. I thought you were just doing this for show," she confessed.

"Really?"

"Yeah. I thought that at the very end, you would just give the baby back over to the mother. You know, once you got what you wanted, which is TV time, you'd dip and that'd be the end of that," Claire explained frankly.

"Wow. That's some hypothesis you have." He was taken aback by her candor.

"Of course now I don't think that anymore. I see a different side of you. I have to ask you, though." She paused and took a breath before voicing this next question. "You seem to want a child really badly. So surely you've tried with someone in the past, right?"

He hesitated a bit, not knowing if Claire was deserving enough of the truth. After all, she was still technically a stranger to him. “Um…yeah, I’ve actually tried with several people. But uh…things didn’t work out in my favor.” He swallowed as he braced himself for what he was about to say next. “I came to the realization that…people just wanted me for my money. And then too, when my parents died, something clicked in my brain—”

“Hey!” Stan shouted, walking back over to Claire and Harvey. “You guys aren’t having a deep conversation without being mic’ed, are you? We know that’s a big no-no.”

They both stared at him dumbfounded and exchanged guilty looks. “Sorry,” Harvey apologized.

Stan shook his head in a reprimanding way. “If I was a prick, I’d totally dock your guys’ pay, but I’m not a mean person. Talking without a wire is a serious offense, truly it is. Especially if it’s juicy stuff like what you guys were talking about. I just heard the tail end of it, but it sounded like something that would’ve given *a lot* to the storyline. Please don’t let it happen again.” Harvey and Claire looked down shamefacedly like students who just got chastised by the teacher. “Next time, just wait to get wired and then you can say whatever you want. Or if it burns you that bad to get if off your chest, just ask a production assistant to mic you. We might not be able to film you at that particular moment, but as long as we have audio—"

"So you can sound bite us?" Harvey interrupted.

"You know this business all too well, kid." Stan teasingly punched him in the shoulder.

*****

Stan was relieved that he was able to find at least one other filming location for the day. Now he'd be able to rest easy tonight. He had found a nice little sitting area just in front of a gigantic fountain in Santusca Park. It wasn't the most ideal place to shoot, but it was a place nonetheless and that's all he cared about. If they could just get the Godforsaken seagulls away from the vicinity, they could start taping. The crew had been battling the flying nuisances for a good thirty minutes, once again, leaving the stars Claire and Harvey waiting. Harvey repeatedly tapped his knee with his fingers while Claire's leg bounced around hyperactively. Their patience was running thin, and the bags of clothes Claire had were an added aggravation.

“C’mon, Stan. Let’s get this show on the road, before Claire and I have another off-camera convo,” Harvey poked.

“Oh, I’m not worried about that this time, smart guy,” Stan said, shooing away one of the white devils that landed on an idle microphone boom. “You guys are mic’ed this time, so we can still catch what you say.”

“Oh yeah? Well what if we did *this* with no camera around?” Harvey grabbed Claire’s face and gave her a big, wet kiss. Her eyes doubled their size.

Stan immediately whipped around to see what Harvey did. “You’re funny, Harvey. Real funny.”

Harvey guffawed. “Don’t test us, Mr. Garagiola. You need us in order for this show to air, right?” All Stan could do was just look at him and roll his eyes. Checkmated.

The other producer, Brent, came over to let everyone know that they would start recording in four minutes. The seagulls just wouldn’t let up, so they had to make the best of the situation and edit the birds out later. The crew took their places, and Claire and Harvey were told to look natural. Funny how they had to snap back into looking normal after having done seven takes of a simple walk-up to the sitting area. At least they were able to continuously shoot the exit from Joveni without hearing “Cut!” yelled at them every few steps.

“Okay, so you guys know what you’re gonna talk about. Let the communication flow. I’m gonna try not to disrupt as much as possible. Have at it, folks.” Stan ran to his position behind the main camera and jammed his eye into the viewfinder. He held up his hand, counted down from five on his fingers, and pointed to Claire and Harvey. Two camera guys stood on either side of the two.

“I can’t thank you enough for getting these clothes for me, Harvey. They’re really cute.” Claire pulled a pink top out of a bag and held it up against her chest.

“You’re gonna look beautiful in them.” Harvey smiled. He stared into her eyes thoughtfully. “You know you have a very unique glow about you?” He rested his chin on his hand dreamily.

Claire was speechless, glancing around shyly for something to say back.

“I’m sorry, I didn’t mean to—”

"No, no, I'm just…at a loss for words," Claire said. She saw Stan out the corner of her eye, motioning for her to keep the dialogue going. "You're a really sweet guy," she said quietly. Then she paused, wanting to revisit the conversation they had at the store a couple of hours ago. But she hesitated, feeling that it wouldn't make sense to discuss something that hadn't been previously recorded. In her periphery, she could see Stan itching to get involved, and this increased the nervousness she was feeling. Something inside her was telling her to pick up where she and Harvey left off. In that instance, she couldn't imagine talking about anything else. She had to know what Harvey was going to say before he was cut off by Stan.

She didn't care about a production or what made sense for TV. She was just going to come out and say what she wanted, because this was *her* reality. "Harvey…when your parents died, what clicked in your brain?"

For five straight minutes, there was dead silence. One of the camera guys stopped filming and put his camera down, looking at the producers in sheer confusion. For the first time, Stan had nothing to say. Harvey froze. He wanted to express his approval for her breaking the rules and being authentic, but didn't want to upset Stan in any way.

He drew in a large breath and shakily let it go, preparing himself to answer her question. He resolved in his mind that he would entertain this conversation again, regardless of how any of the producers felt about it. Because this was *his* reality.

"When my parents died…something clicked in my brain that I could never get close to anyone ever again. It's like… from that point forward, I felt that forming relationships was pointless. But I still tried anyway, ya know?"

"Have you ever been able to love anyone?" Claire asked, tenderly putting her hand over his.

"Not like I want to. I've been with so many different women, Claire. And none of them worked out for me." He exhaled heavily. "Now I'm thirty years old, and I'm at that stage where it's like, what's the point in trying anymore? Significant others are overrated. I still want my child, though. That's one thing I told my parents I would definitely accomplish, and I'm not gonna let even myself get in the way of that, you know what I mean?"

Claire nodded understandingly. But if she hadn't felt bad before, she certainly felt bad now about not actually being pregnant. Harvey was nice enough to choose her, thinking that she was the best candidate to be the mother of his child. All he wanted was a kid. That's all he wanted. No romantic attachments, no friend with benefits, none of that. Just someone he could call his offspring. And Claire was not currently in a position to give that to him. It almost brought her to tears to know that she misled this guy. She could care less about pulling one over on the producers. But this man, someone with a genuine soul. She could never forgive herself for hurting him. She had to hold it together for now, though. It was still too early to come clean, she thought.

But as much as Harvey implied that getting a child was his primary intent for signing up for the show, Claire surmised that there was more to it than that. The way he looked at her, not just her, but the other ladies that were competing as well. When he delivered his speeches to each of them, the manner in which he described them and their qualities, Claire could tell that he wanted more than just a surrogate mother. He wanted someone to love. And hearing about his past confirmed that.

Stan stormed from behind the camera and over to Claire, wearing the tensest face you could ever imagine. How he managed to contort his features into such an unsettling position was beyond Claire. "Okay, dear. We need to reset this conversation because how did we go from talking about maternity clothes to failed relationships? This isn't Dr. Phil, honey. I'm sorry if I'm coming off abrasive, but you have to remember, there's a certain look that this show needs to have." He flared his nostrils angrily and stomped back over to the camera, which was adjacent to a flat monitor. "Let me show you something, Claire."

She reluctantly got up and went over to where he was. "Come look at this screen. Stand right next to me," he ordered. She obliged and looked at the screen which was divided into four equal squares. Each corresponded to a particular camera and was respectively labeled A, B, C, and D. He pointed to square D and hit a button on a keyboard that was attached to the monitor. The last five minutes of footage was being played back. He hurried up and grabbed a pair of headphones, gesturing for her to put them on so she could hear. But she could barely hear anything. The speech was muffled. She could only see the numbers at the bottom of the square rapidly going and her and Harvey moving around.

"I can't hear it," she said.

Stan promptly turned up the volume. "I want you to look at this footage and tell me if this scene makes sense."

She stared intently at the screen, reliving the last five minutes of her life captured on film. After only a minute or so of watching it, she yanked the headphones off. "Does it really matter? All you have to do is edit some clips together so it makes sense. Use your little sound clips and stuff and throw it in where you think it'll make the story clearer."

"Honey, it doesn't always work like that. Editors can only do so much to make the footage coherent," Stan explicated. "You guys agreed to talk about the maternity clothes, future plans, and that was it. You just threw everyone for a loop."

"Well this is reality, Stan. Don't you want our interactions to be organic? Neither myself nor Harvey wanted to talk about some stupid clothes." Claire felt her temperature starting to rise little by little. She took a breath to bring herself down a few notches. "Look, if me talking about *real* issues is gonna be a problem for you, then maybe you should look for another female lead."

Chapter 4

Claire was resistant to the idea of sitting down with Stan over a cup of coffee and discussing what had happened the other day. She didn't want to talk about it anymore, but Stan insisted that they hash it out, so she agreed. Besides, she kind of had no other choice but to stay and do the show since she had quit her job. It wouldn't hurt to at least hear Stan out, especially if it meant not ending up homeless. Regardless, she was still leery about meeting with him, and demanded that cameras or microphones or anything else production-related not even be present with her around. Stan honored her request and assured her that it would just be him and her.

The two of them decided to visit Jemma's Java Haus, a cozy little coffee shop on Cloverdale Street. Stan invited Claire to get whatever she wanted off the menu on his dime, a gesture that confirmed to her that he *was* trying to make amends. Things had gotten uglier after he chastised her about derailing the planned conversation during shooting. She threatened to quit the show, going on a tirade about how fabricated reality TV was and how producers exploit people. And he countered everything she said with, "Well, this is how the industry is, honey. Take it or leave it." He even destroyed her ego when he told her point blank that she could easily be replaced. That comment bothered him, which prompted him to extend the olive branch.

In truth, he knew that no one could replace Claire. Not because she was a one of a kind personality, but because it was too late to find someone else to fill her slot. They were already well into the filming schedule, and it would be a huge hassle on production to scrap all footage of Claire and start from scratch. And they would have to start *all* the way over, more than likely having to bring in a whole new batch of ladies for Harvey to choose from. That would drastically push the premiere date back, which would cause the network to lose money, which in turn, would make Stan and the rest of the production company be out of a job. So this coffee meeting was nothing more than damage control. But Stan did genuinely feel bad about how he handled Claire, and grew to respect her enough to set things straight. Most producers wouldn't even bat an eye about the situation, in spite of how backed into a corner they are.

"Got what you wanted?" Stan asked, cradling his cup of espresso as the steam ascended up to his glasses and fogged them.

"Oh yes, thanks," Claire replied, timidly swirling her coffee around with her finger. She acted as if she didn't want it. But the truth of the matter was, she was just apprehensive about how Stan would behave. He was a bit of a wild card sometimes, and you could kind of tell just by how erratic he looked.

"Okay now. Don't ask for a croissant or a donut when we get ready to leave," he joked. "You sure you're not hungry? I thought you skipped breakfast this morning."

"I did. I can't really eat when I'm nervous," she explained quietly.

"Nervous? About this? We're just two friends having a normal conversation."

A jolt of irritation went through Claire's body. *No, we're not friends*, she thought. *So how dare you say that. This is strictly business. I would never be friends with someone like you outside of this.*

She really wanted to say what she was thinking, but didn't want to turn the mood sour. Instead, she softly chuckled to conceal her true feelings. "There's just something on my chest that I need to get off." She looked at Stan seriously. He returned a worried look.

"Well, before you tell me, I just want to, again…reiterate my apologies to you. I didn't mean to come off so brusque. But, what I wanted you to understand is that as a supervising producer, I have a job to do. And that's to ensure that production is executed effectively and consistently. When we have abrupt changes in story arcs, like what we had the other day, if there's no footage or information to tie everything together, it won't make any sense. Can you understand that aspect of it?" He eased his hands closer to Claire's as if he was about to affectionately touch them. She politely scooted her hands back to avoid his. If he thought that would somehow disarm her, he had another thing coming, she thought.

"Yes, I understand the production side of it. But what I was trying to get *you* to see is the *character* side of it. And I hate to use that word 'character,' because it implies that we're one-dimensional. We're not really characters, Stan. We're real people with real stories, real emotions, and since this is 'reality

TV'—" She air quoted the last two words. "—we should be allowed the liberty to express ourselves authentically. Now how you guys choose to edit that is your business, but at least give us the freedom to live our truth on camera. You get where I'm coming from?"

Stan nodded contemplatively. Everything she said was really making an impression on him. Not only because it was true and insightful, but because no cast member who worked for him had ever been bold enough to be frank with him. Even the most headstrong personalities he worked with in the past wouldn't have the gall to do what Claire did. And she did it with such maturity and class, too.

"Claire, I hear you. I truly do. And that's one thing that I would like to bring to the attention of the network someday. They're really the ones who dictate the image of the show, they're the final authority. But hopefully, we can make some progress in the future, and try to get better exposure for those who put their lives in front of the world." Stan seemed sincere in what he was saying, but Claire wasn't totally buying it. She kind of felt like he was just telling her what she wanted to hear, just to pacify her for the time being.

Claire chuckled again. “Stan, I do accept your apology though.” She let out a reluctant sigh. “I’m not goin’ anywhere. I need this job just as much as you need yours, so…let’s finish this thing strong.”

“Alright, that’s what I like to hear!” The biggest grin spread across Stan’s face as he threw his hand in the air for a high five from her. She tapped his hand unenthusiastically with a cool smirk.

A waitress came over to see if they needed anything, which dispelled the awkward moment that Claire created just then. “How are you guys doing over here? Can I get you something?” She was a sweet, young twenty-something with dark red hair and glasses. Looked like a good-natured college student just trying to make ends meet.

“No thanks, sweetheart, we’re fine,” Stan answered.

“Okay, well if you guys change your mind, just holler.” She gave the warmest smile and tended back to her barista position.

“Now, were you gonna tell me something else?” Stan asked, noisily gulping down some espresso.

"Oh, um…yeah, there's something serious I really need to talk to you about."

"Is it something I'm not gonna wanna hear, or?"

"Well, to be honest, yes."

"Oh boy." That worried look came back to his face.

"I have to tell you this, Stan. If I'm gonna move forward with you on this show, I have to tell you this. It's crucial." There was a very heavy silence that descended on the table.

"Okay, please spit it out. My nerves are on edge," Stan said, feverishly scratching his scalp .

Claire couldn't believe she was actually about to do this, right here, right now. But there was no better opportunity than now to lay the truth on the table. She had just somewhat reconciled with Stan, and he deserved to know the truth. But she feared that it might set him off and throw him back three steps, and their resolution would've been for naught. Then she started thinking about Harvey and what this would mean for him. She already reasoned in her mind that pulling a fast one on producers isn't nearly as unethical as pulling one on a cast mate. So she would go ahead and reveal the truth on Harvey's account, not because of some bonehead producer.

"Stan," she began, her hands nervously folding into each other. Her mouth kept opening and closing as she wrestled with whether or not she should tell him. Then she forced herself to think about Harvey again. She needed to at least do this for him if nothing else. "Stan, um…I'm not pregnant."

Stan was mid-sip when she came out and said it, and nearly spit out his coffee. Instead, he swallowed it down like a brick. It took him a moment to regroup. "I'm sorry, you're not *what*?" His tone was biting and it honestly struck a little fear in Claire.

"I'm not pregnant," she repeated, this time with less unease. Stan silently folded his arms and gave her a drilling gaze expecting her to explain herself. "I signed up for this show because I really needed the money. My teaching job wasn't really supporting my lifestyle like I wanted, and I needed an out. So when this came along, I jumped on the opportunity." All while she was saying this, she was staring down at her coffee trying her hardest to avert eye contact with Stan. She felt shameful.

"So…you couldn't apply for another show? That actually fits your reality? I mean, out of all the casting calls in the world, you just happen to find us and try to be on *our* show, knowing full well that you're not a lick of pregnant? And I remember clear as day, our casting call specifically asking for women who were no more than two to three weeks pregnant. I know, because I wrote it and posted it. I honestly feel swindled right now." He buried his head in his hands and took a few long breaths. "It just boggles me…that you were even able to advance through the audition rounds without getting found out, like…so when the casting producers asked you for proof of pregnancy, i.e., a pregnancy test, what did you do? Steal some random pregnant woman's test?" Now he was being sarcastic, and Claire detected that. Could she blame him though?

"No. At the time, my friend took one and hers turned up positive, and so I asked to borrow it for the show," she admitted.

"Wow. I've seen people go to some crazy extremes just to be on TV, but this…this is way up there. This isn't the worst I've seen, but it's pretty darn nuts nonetheless. Your friend should've been the one on here, then! How far along was she?"

"She was about two and a half weeks, I believe."

"Hmm. What's she like?" Stan leaned in, curious about this mystery woman.

"She's a very nice, sweet girl. Never really gets out much. She just handles her own and tries to live a quiet life."

"Well, that's boring," Stan said bluntly. "Maybe she wouldn't have been a good fit for the show."

"But her story is real, and that should be what matters, not how exciting or exuberant her life is."

"Listen, we're not gonna talk about that, okay? In the meantime, what I'm gonna do is pay for you to get an artificial insemination. There's no ifs, ands, or buts about it. Matter of fact, instead of tapping into our budget which is really tight right now, I'm gonna take it out of your paycheck."

Claire's head jerked back in surprise and Stan looked at her as if to say "you have no right to be shocked at this. This is all your doing anyway and these are the repercussions." She picked up her porcelain mug and swirled around her coffee, pondering what she would say next.

"I feel like this is a violation of my rights. So you're gonna *actually* impregnate me to make this legit?"

"Absolutely, sweetheart. We have to make this real. Months from now, we'll be filming your ultrasound, and then months after that, the delivery of the baby. And it's gonna be a raw, up close, and personal moment with very little editing. We're gonna capture every moment of the childbirth, especially your reactions. So yes, you need to have a *real* baby."

Claire looked around worriedly. She wasn't ready to have a baby, definitely not under these circumstances. She just wanted to come on the show, earn her pay, and go back to regular life. But did she really think she'd be able to squirm her way out of the unavoidable? Like actually *showing*, getting an ultrasound, and the eventual birth? There's no way she could've been that shortsighted to not foresee how this could crumble in front of her face. But she *was* that shortsighted. She only thought in immediate terms when she applied for the show, thinking about the amount of money she would get and how cool it would be just to be on TV.

She exhaled and braced herself for what she was about to say. “Okay, Stan. If that’s what you want, then that’s what I’ll do,” she yielded to his stipulation. “I made my bed, so now I have to lie in it. What clinic am I going to?”

“I’ll have to look for one. And I’m glad you see things my way. Claire, think about it. This is a surrogate mother show after all, right? I know you might be averse to the idea of being pregnant, but all you have to do is power through these next nine months, have the baby, give it to Harvey, and move on with your life. I’m not asking you to keep it and raise it for eighteen years and send it off to college.” Stan chortled. “And of course, this secret stays between us, alright? You’re *not* gonna tell Harvey. Is that understood?”

Claire looked at him with uncertainty. “I’m not sure I can agree to that. He deserves to know just as much as you.”

“Claire, if you tell him, that’s gonna disrupt the flow of the storyline. ‘Cause in the back of his mind, all he’s gonna think about is the fact that you lied to him. And that's gonna create some weird tension that the audience won't know about. Again, we gotta keep stuff consistent." He paused to think. "Unless you decide to tell him after the show wraps. That's the only time I'll let you do it," Stan said. "But you know what, that could work perfectly, because then we'll have a point of conflict for the reunion special," he muttered to himself.

"What's that?" Claire asked.

"Oh, don't mind me, I'm just thinking out loud. Hey, since you're back on board to continue with the show, where do you think we should go from here?"

"As far as…"

"As far as the direction of the show, the themes we have going so far, the issues we're highlighting. Do you think we should change anything? What should we bring attention to?"

"Honestly, Stan, I feel like what we've shot so far is kinda shallow. There's no substance there or anything that viewers can really relate to. At least that's what it seems like from my vantage point."

"Well see, this is why when we were at Joveni the other day, I was irked to see you and Harvey having that conversation without being mic'ed. It sounded really deep and something that would've added weight to the storyline."

"So why didn't you just ask us to talk about it again, then?"

"Because, using your words, it wouldn't seem organic. The emotion behind it wouldn't have been natural. The whole dialogue would've seemed forced. And I couldn't ask Harvey to revisit those emotions, first of all, out of respect for his feelings. I didn't want him to have to peel back that scab again just for the sake of good TV. And secondly, me asking him to do that is akin to a director asking an actor to put themselves in a certain state of mind for a scene. This isn't a movie or a sitcom. Just because I can sometimes have a cinematic vision doesn't mean I can't differentiate reality from scripted."

Claire was taken aback that Stan was capable of being ethical. "Okay, that makes perfect sense."

"So to make this show more substantial, what else can we bring to the forefront that's raw and authentic? Is there something about Harvey, or yourself, that we can delve into? Personality flaws, deep-rooted problems, past conflicts?"

Claire had a precise answer ready. "Harvey's views on love. He doesn't think that it's possible for him to foster a relationship. Part of that is due to the loss of his parents, but it also stems from women just getting with him for his money. So it's like, overall, he just thinks love is futile."

"Okay, good. We can work with that," Stan said, taking a sip of espresso. It seemed like he was slipping back into callous producer mode, as he appeared to be more interested in how this story could benefit the show rather than the story itself.

"I don't know where you plan on filming next, but wherever we do it, I think I wanna have a conversation with him about this."

"So how are you gonna approach it?" Stan waved over the young waitress from before as he leaned in to Claire with all ears.

*****

Claire and Harvey sat out on her balcony overlooking the river behind the apartment building. They were wearing wires and a camera guy was standing a few feet away from them, filming their conversation. It was a bit nerve-racking since the balcony wasn't that big and could barely accommodate two people, let alone three. But Stan and his "vision" called for them to be casually enjoying a breezy, overcast day at home. A few times, the cameraman almost went tumbling over the edge when he failed to gauge how far back he was walking. He kept telling Stan that the shot was too close, but Stan insisted that he just keep filming.

"Harvey, you do realize that there are plenty of women out there who don't just get with you for your fame, or your money, or your looks, right?"

"Oh yeah? Well why does *every* single one I come across do just that? And I'm talking women that I've dated exclusively, *and* women I was just talking to. They were all the same."

"Harvey, you *can* find love if you just look for it in the right person—"

"Oh please, Claire. Don't butter me up with that cliché bologna. You know as well as I do that with *me* in particular, chicks are just after the moolah. Half the time, I don't think they even care about my looks. Nowadays, you can be butt ugly and still snag a female, as long as your bank account looks like a phone number."

Claire laughed. "Like half of these rappers out today? And heck, some of these athletes too. I mean, severely busted in the face, but still have the prettiest broads on their arms." She chuckled again.

"See? And I have way more money than those guys. Claire, you're only supporting my point."

"But Harvey, every woman alive isn't a gold digger, or an opportunist, or superficial. I know there are plenty of women out there who would love to be with you for *you*. You have an interesting personality and a real story. A little conceited sometimes, but you're not a bad guy." They both laughed. "Seriously, though. The right one will come along. You just have to be patient."

"I hear what you're saying, Claire. But what if that right one never shows up? What if because of my status, I just get a never-ending stream of gold diggers for the rest of my life? And there's gonna be that one that I end up married to, and when I expire, she's gonna take me for everything I'm worth. I just have to face the fact that since I'm so wealthy, I'll forever be a gold digger magnet."

"Patience is key, Harvey. You may never find someone in this lifetime, but that's okay. We weren't put on this earth to fall in love. Our sole purpose was to procreate and enjoy the fruits of the earth. Love is just an added luxury from God."

"My patience is wearing thin," he replied solemnly.

"Okay. The Bible says at First Corinthians, chapter thirteen, and verse four that love is long-suffering or patient. That's literally the first sentence of the verse. Meditate on that, please do. Even if you don't believe in the Bible, it still puts things into perspective."

"Yeah, well I'm not sure how a book written thousands of years ago by *men* is supposed to help me now. So…I think I'm done with this conversation." With that, Harvey got up to go back in the apartment.

Claire was left sitting there, not humiliated for how he responded, but instead, she truly hoped in her heart that he would see the wisdom of that inspired word. At any rate, her work was not done. If Harvey didn't want to be patient with his love life, she would be patient with him.

Chapter 5

It had been almost three months since filming began, and Claire was starting to develop feelings for Harvey. She thought she'd never fall for a guy like him, but the more she spent time with him, the more she grew to enjoy his company. He wasn't nearly as self-centered or pompous as he portrayed himself to be. Claire determined that that was probably a social mask he wore until he got to know you on a deeper level. Because now, he was comfortable enough to be himself, which was a gentle, sensitive, and thoughtful man. She concluded that the loss of his parents made him become a guarded individual and for good reason. He had to have some type of barrier for the women who wanted to come into his life just for his money.

Harvey didn't think he'd ever catch feelings in this situation; his intent was merely to come on and meet a suitable woman to carry his baby. Nothing more, nothing less. But now he was forming something for Claire he didn't think possible. The two of them were secretly trying to resist their true feelings for one another. However, with each day spent together, the mutual chemistry was becoming increasingly harder to fight. And Claire's raging hormones from the baby weren't making it any easier.

The two were walking down Selleck Avenue in Calabasas, thankfully with no cameras or microphones around to capture their every move. Today was a "down day" where they could do whatever they wanted without having to answer to a producer. They could finally have a conversation and not feel guilty about whether it was caught on record. It was nice to go back to normalcy for a bit.

"I have to stop in this school for a minute. Wanna come with me?" Harvey asked.

"Going to enroll the baby this early?" Claire teased.

Harvey laughed a little. "No. Mr. DeLosche has been my mentor since childhood. He's slated to make an appearance on the show, actually. I just wanna say hello."

"Sure, okay," Claire agreed.

They ascended the concrete steps leading to the front door. The place was quite regal-looking for an elementary and middle school and gave off the vibe that it was the type of institution where you would want your child to go.

Mr. DeLosche was just finishing up a conversation with a gentleman when he spotted Harvey entering the auditorium. "Har-vey! Ha ha ha!" His face turned bright red with glee when he saw his former student. They embraced each other as Mr. DeLosche heartily patted Harvey's back. "It's so good to see ya." It became apparent that he had a slight Irish accent. "I was so glad to hear that you might be coming by. Aha, it's been way too long." He turned to Claire. "I've known him since he was ye high." He lowered his hand all the way down just above his knee. "He would sneak into the girls' bathroom when everyone had gone to class and hide under the sink so he could take pictures of legs." Claire laughed, while Harvey shamefully pinched the bridge of his nose and tried to bury his face from any human contact. He couldn't help but laugh himself, though.

"Here, sit, please sit," he offered, gesturing towards the seats in the front row. He pulled up a folding chair that was sitting off to the side. "Ohh, look at the two of you." Mr. DeLosche deliberately eased his bottom down. "Such a beautiful couple." Claire and Harvey exchanged looks, smiling to repel any awkwardness.

"I must say, Harvey. You sure know how to pick 'em." He perused Claire's form almost perversely, shaking his head rapidly to take himself out of the immoral thoughts that crept their way into his head. Claire caught on and pressed her legs tightly together, politely angling her body away from him.

"Uhh, Mr. DeLosche, we aren't—" Harvey tried to explain.

"I find the most attractive partners to be interracial. There's just something about the union of two people who come from different backgrounds that truly underscores the beauty of unconditional love. I truly delight to see interracial couples."

"Mr. DeLosche, let me explain. We're not a couple," Harvey said.

"Okay, well you guys are *talking*, or whatever new-age term they use nowadays. Talking, dating, same difference," Mr. DeLosche replied dismissively.

Claire laughed awkwardly. "No, no, you don't understand. We're basically strangers to each other," Harvey clarified.

"We're all strangers initially, Harvey. It takes a lifetime to get to know someone. That's the beauty of a relationship. Each day you're with that person, you find another reason why you chose them," Mr. DeLosche said.

Claire laughed awkwardly again and turned to Harvey. "Harvey, may I?" she asked him. Maybe *she* could get him to understand. Mr. DeLosche was well along in age, and thus could only comprehend things that sounded the closest to old-fashioned norms. Or at least things that were to the point.

"Mr. DeLosche, um, we're…essentially coworkers," Claire said simply.

"Lots of people find their future mates at their place of work," he responded. Claire and Harvey looked at each other again, thinking that at this point, there was no getting through to him. "Let me tell you the story of how I met my second wife of seventeen years. Before I worked here at this school, I used to clean cubicles at the DeWalt office building in downtown—Oh no, no, that was my first girlfriend." Claire and Harvey silently exchanged amusement. “Have you two slept together?”

Claire’s eyes doubled their size. “No, Mr. DeLosche!”

“Sorry, I just had to know. I was going to say, once you guys lock into each other, you’ve already started something serious. Just saying.” He held up his hands in innocence.

“Mr. DeLosche, this is Claire. We met about three months ago via that TV show that I want you to make a cameo on. Claire is the woman I chose to be the surrogate mother of my baby,” Harvey explained.

“Oh yesss!” Mr. DeLosche finally caught on. He sniggered ashamedly. “I apologize for being presumptuous. You two just seemed like a couple to me, so I assumed.”

“No. Claire and I are just…friends,” Harvey said.

“Friends. See, my instincts would tell me that you guys were an item, especially knowing that she’s carrying your child. But I gotcha.”

“Mr. DeLosche, we don’t wanna keep you.” They all stood at once. “I just wanted to see you, and…it means a lot that you'll be coming onto the show." He shook Mr. DeLosche's hand.

"I wouldn't miss it," he replied. He turned to shake Claire's hand. "And it was a pleasure meeting you, Claire. Oh, and I believe I'm supposed to come on in two weeks or something like that? A producer phoned me about it the other day, but it must've slipped my mind."

"Alright, Mr. DeLosche. We'll be seeing you," Harvey said, as Claire started for the exit. He followed right behind.

"Let's Make a Baby! That's the name of the show I'm supposed to be on, right? Ugh, boy I tell you, being old and forgetful is no fun, kids, take my word for it!" Claire and Harvey chuckled. "I just want to tell you one last thing. Ya know, sometimes, it's the very people we least expect who are the ones we're most compatible with. There might even be a twinkling of something that you might dismiss. But that little something could very well be a spark of love. Don't ignore or resist it, folks. You two enjoy each other's company. And I'll see you in two weeks."

"Thank you, Mr. DeLosche," Claire said continuing towards the door.

Claire and Harvey exited the building, a hint of tension evident in their not saying anything to each other. Mr. DeLosche's words hung on their hearts.

"I gotta go, Harvey," she said, folding her arms.

"Yeah, me too," he responded.

"I'll see you later." Claire left at once, flagging down a taxi.

"See you later," Harvey said, with somewhat of a sad expression on his face.

*****

"How's the show going, dear?" Geraldine asked Claire, taking a sip of tea. "You haven't told me anything about it since you started filming!" Claire and her mom went to a quaint little restaurant called Bev's to catch up and have lunch.

"Mom, I can't really reveal too much about the show because I could get fired. I'm not really supposed to leak information, not even to close family members," Claire said with an attitude.

“Honey, who am I going to tell? I’m over sixty years old, I barely know anyone who watches what’s on TV these days.”

Claire rolled her eyes. She knew her mom was just trying to be nosy and get the inside scoop. “Mom, you’re just a quidnunc,” she said flatly.

Geraldine jerked her head back. She had no idea what that word meant or implied. “What did you call me, young lady?” Her voice elevated.

Claire chortled. “Mom, a quidnunc is a person who likes to hear the latest gossip. They thrive on hearing drama and mess. We all know that’s you in a nutshell, ma.”

“Girl, I ain’t no quiz-nun, or quip-monk, or whatever you just called me. It sounds you like just hurled one of them British slang words at me. Long as you don’t call me no tallywacker.”

Claire’s face twisted with puzzlement. “What-what even is that?”

“I don’t know, honey, I heard it on the television the other day, though. And the person that got called it got real offended. So that's why I know it's not a good word to call somebody." You could tell Geraldine was an old school type of mother, a mother with Southern values. The kind who takes any remark outside of "Yes, ma'am" as disrespect. She was still learning to rein in her inflexible approach to everything, especially after having moved to California with Claire. She soon learned that her zero tolerance for this and that wouldn't fly out there. People were much more liberated than she was used to.

"Mom, I would never call you something that's disrespectful. You know that," Claire said.

"Alright, now. You betta recognize who I am and what I stand for," Geraldine said firmly. "Where'd that word even come from anyway?"

"I don't know, really. I saw it on Twitter somewhere."

"Who? Twitter? What's that?"

Claire laughed. "Mother, Twitter is a social network where you can write anything you want in about 140 characters. You mean to tell me you've never heard of Twitter? It's been out for almost ten years!"

"Child, that don't mean I know what it is, or even heard of it. If it had been out for fifty years, I probably still wouldn't know what it is. But baby, what's the word? How's this TV show thing working out for ya?"

"It's goin'," Claire answered cryptically.

"Meaning?" Geraldine leaned in, slurping on her tea.

"Meaning that it's running how it should. Everyone's on the same page. Things are copacetic."

"Can I ask you something? Why am I not on the show? I mean, wouldn't it make sense to have the surrogate mother's *own* mother on the show, for moral support? Advice, pointers, words of wisdom for the mom-to-be? I should fit into the story somewhere."

Claire released a sigh chocked full of hesitation. "Mom, Stan, the producer, felt like you wouldn't fit into the storyline. That's just—"

"Wouldn't fit into the storyline?" Geraldine frowned. "Does that make any type of sense? If anything, I should be a staple for the show. He couldn't make me a recurring cast member at least? What kinda mess is he on?"

"Mom, do you just wanna be on TV?" Claire asked, pursing her lips.

"Well, yeah, child! It's always been a dream of mine to grace the small screen," Geraldine admitted, fluffing her hair like a movie star. "I tried to break out into show biz when I was your age. Everybody called me the Black Marilyn Monroe!" She lifted her head proudly.

"Ma, the Black Marilyn Monroe? Did you take your meds this morning? Because you're on one today," Claire joked, covering her mouth from laughing.

"Girl, whatever. So this Harvey kid ...what's he like?"

"He's—he's nice. When I first met him, I thought he was the most egotistical brick head I had ever met. But after getting to know his story, I see a deeper side of him." Claire abruptly went silent, as if she had nothing else to say about him.

"And? There's gotta be more to it than that, babe." Geraldine knew her daughter wasn't telling the full story. "Honey, I've known you for twenty-eight years. You think I don't know when you're not telling me everything?"

Claire remained silent, darting her eyes around the restaurant to avoid eye contact with her mom. Just then, a waitress approached the table with a notepad and pen in hand. She saved Claire from an awkward moment. "You guys ready to order yet?"

"Yes, dear. Let me get the pork chops and gravy with a side of greens and black-eyed peas," Geraldine said, her gaze stubbornly fixed on Claire. She was not going to look elsewhere until her daughter started talking. The waitress perceived tension at the table and it made her anxious to hurry up and get these orders so she could get away.

"O-okay," she stammered. "And for you, ma'am?" She turned to Claire.

"Um...I'll just take a hamburger, medium well with everything on it. With a side of sweet potato fries."

"Alrighty. Anything to drink for you, ma'am?"

"No thanks. I'll stick with my water," Claire replied, raising her glass.

"Okay. Your meals will be out shortly." She grabbed the menus off the table and scurried off to her next duty.

Geraldine had not looked up to acknowledge the waitress once. Her eyes were too busy penetrating Claire's soul. "You know I don't like it when you keep things from me, right? Start talking."

"Mom, there's *nothing* to say. Can you just drop it?" Claire demanded smartly.

"I would if you were paying this bill. But seeing as though that's not the case, I can ask you whatever I want." Claire rolled her eyes and let out an irritated sigh. "Next time, if you don't want mammy to ask certain questions, you can treat. Fair deal?"

Claire sighed again. "Okay. You want the full truth, so here it is. I think that I'm falling for Harvey, Mom."

Geraldine gave her the longest stare. “Claire. You tried to avoid telling me *that*? Girl, what’s there to be embarrassed about?”

“It’s not about being embarrassed, Mom. It’s about not wanting to catch feelings for someone I’m not supposed to.”

“And by ‘not supposed to,’ you mean….”

“This show isn’t really about finding love. It’s merely about a surrogate mother producing a child for a man in desperate want of a child. This isn’t a dating show, Mom.”

“You can’t help who you fall for, baby. You two have been spending lots of time together, so you were bound to catch feelings at some point.”

Claire chuckled sardonically. “Tell that to Harvey.”

“What?”

“I went to his old school with him the other day when we had an off day of filming. And funny thing is, his old teacher thought we were a couple. So as we were trying to explain to him what the situation was, Harvey tells him that we're virtually strangers. So I'm like oh really? That's what our three-month friendship has been reduced to?"

Geraldine hummed disdainfully and ponderingly. "Wonder why he would say that."

"I mean, granted, we haven't known each other that long. But on a show like this, it's like time is stretched, and three months of knowing someone feels like a year. So that's why I was so taken aback by his comment. It's like he just diminished a whole year-long friendship."

"Maybe the reason it offended you so is because there's deeper feelings there that go past just a friendship, dear."

Claire's heart stopped abruptly. She knew her mom was telling the truth, but she couldn't bring herself to outwardly express that.

"Trust me, hun. I know when a gal's in love. And is trying to hide it," Geraldine continued.

"Honestly, I think that if there *is* anything for him, it's due to the hormones."

"Oh, don't go finding reasons for why you feel the way you feel. Okay yeah, the hormones, but in my opinion, sweetheart, they can't affect what's not there to begin with. You obviously have some kind of affinity for this man, and the hormones are merely amplifying that. Don't play ya mama. I may have been born *at* night, but I wasn't born *last* night."

Claire looked down solemnly, attempting to sort out her feelings. The waitress had returned with their food. "Here you guys go. Enjoy!"

"Thanks," Claire and Geraldine said in unison, as their server smiled and headed over to the next table.

Suddenly, Claire's phone rang. She immediately unzipped her purse which was hanging on the side of her chair to retrieve it. Anything to get away from this conversation about Harvey.

And ironically enough, it was him who was calling. She nervously glanced at her mom, somehow thinking that she would psychically know who it was. The phone kept ringing.

"Aren't you gonna answer that?" Geraldine asked suspiciously.

Claire looked back at her phone and reluctantly swiped to accept the call. “H-hello?”

“Hey, Claire. I know the last time we saw each other, we kinda ended things on a weird note. What was that even about? Did I say something wrong?”

Claire wanted so badly to tell him how she felt about his “strangers” comment, but then her mom would know instantly who she was talking to. Her chest tightened a little from the angst she was feeling.

“N-no, I was just…ready to go. That’s all.” She looked at her mom, who was scrunching up her face trying to decipher who was on the other end.

“Oh okay, I was just curious. I just want you to know, though, that if I ever say or do anything to offend you or rub you wrong, let me know. You know we can always be open and transparent with each other, okay?”

“Yeah,” Claire replied shortly.

“You sure you’re alright? You seem kinda tense.”

“I’m fine.”

"Alright, if you say so. 'Cause I don't want you acting weird on me, too. I've noticed within the past few days how production's been acting kinda strange."

"Really? How so?" Claire's interest was piqued.

"Not returning phone calls, no word from Stan on the scenes he wants us to shoot, no updates on the filming schedule. It's like... they're purposely avoiding me or something. They've just been sort of elusive lately."

"Hmm. I wonder what that's about." Claire gave a slightly fretful look to Geraldine.

"I don't know, but something tells me production might have something stupid up their sleeve. And whatever it is, they want us to be genuinely surprised. That's why they aren't saying much."

"Ugh, that's the last thing I need is surprises. Do they not understand I'm with child?"

"They better understand it because I'll go off if they do anything to jeopardize my baby's well-being." He went silent for a while. Claire shifted the phone to a better position as she waited for him to say something else. She waited patiently. Geraldine's patience, on the other hand, was wearing thin. She obviously couldn't make out what was being said, but she could tell that this mystery person had just suddenly stopped talking. And she wanted them to hurry up and continue so she could ask who it was when Claire hung up.

"Claire, I've really been thinking about you for the past couple days. I don't want you to say anything. Just listen to me. I kept thinking about what Mr. DeLosche said, and....it really struck a nerve with me. Claire, I can't keep bottling up these feelings I have for you. Claire ...I love you."

A tight knot formed inside Claire's throat. The world halted momentarily. She felt like she was slowly falling out of reality. The present was gradually pulling away from her. The ambient buzz of people talking, the clinking of dishes and silverware, her mom calling out her name all became faint blips of sound. It's like she was being submerged under water.

"Claire . . . you still there?" Her phone slipped down from her ear, but her hand was still grasping it somewhat. Geraldine was finally able to hear that it was a man's voice. "Claire?"

"Claire!" Geraldine yelled, attracting the attention of a few surrounding patrons. Claire came to. She immediately looked at the phone and saw that Harvey was still on the line. Still not wanting her mom to see, she promptly ended the call.

"Who was *that*, honey?"

Chapter 6

Claire paced back and forth in her living room as she waited for Harvey to call her back. She was definitely on edge having not heard from producers in over a week. Did they cancel the show without alerting anybody? Had they somehow found a replacement surrogate (which the idea itself was both redundant and ironic)? Did someone on the crew kick the bucket, which caused them to suspend production? What in the world was going on? So many questions and not enough answers. Paranoia was beginning to set in with Claire, and those hormones only exacerbated her mental anguish.

Her face was growing hot with each passing minute that she didn't hear from anybody. Beads of sweat cascaded down her forehead. Her heart wasn't racing per se, but it was beating sporadically, waiting for that one, dreaded moment to go into shock and just stop altogether. She needed to calm down. Not hearing word from Stan, or Brent, or any other personnel from the show did not mean the end of the world. But it was very odd to say the least.

Harvey had told her the other day that he suspected something strange was going on with the producers. He planted a small seed of doubt in her mind about them, but she just wrote it off as a misunderstanding on his end. She figured there had to be a valid explanation as to why they were M.I.A. But now, Claire began to find some legitimacy in Harvey's suspicions. That's why she decided to call him. He didn't answer, so she had to leave a voice message. And that was over thirty minutes ago, which is the reason she was acting so antsy. She wanted to talk to him right away. The uncertainty was driving her nuts.

Realizing that she was stressing over something that could very well be trivial, Claire stopped mid-pace, closed her eyes, took a few calm breaths, and massaged her stomach. She didn't need to be this worked up, because it wasn't healthy for the baby. If Harvey was to see her distressed like this, he would demand that she sit down and pull herself together for the sake of the child. Claire walked over to her recliner and eased down into it, grabbing the remote that was on the end table next to her.

"Maybe some TV can take my mind off of this," she said to herself, closing her eyes tightly and popping them open again. She soon realized the irony of what she just said.

Watching TV to distract her from the anxieties of a TV show she was on.

Claire continued rubbing her stomach, as the picture faded in on her 60-inch, high definition screen. She had left the TV on the Nature Channel, which was currently airing a program all about mothers protecting their young in the animal kingdom. It was an hour-long special, featuring a wide range of creatures from lionesses defending their cubs, to alligator moms going after predators who threatened their eggs, to gorillas avenging the death of their babies. Claire caught it when they were showing a vixen growling at a hunter who got too close to her fox pups.

"...this fox mother is not shy in trying to ward off the danger that faces her innocent litter," an English narrator said over footage of baby foxes cowering in the den.

Claire took a moment to admire the lengths mothers in the wild will go to to care for their offspring. The fact that it's instinctual, that they do it because that's just how they're wired. *And here in the human world,* she mused, *we're so complicated, weighing options and thinking about consequences. Animals don't think, they just do. Sure they lack the intelligent capacity that humans have, but they have unconditional love for their babies. Why can't we be a little more like them?*

"...and once again, she has managed to scare away a potential threat," the narrator continued. Claire wondered which animal she would take a cue from when the baby was born. But then it dawned on her that she wouldn't be able to demonstrate anything she learned from these nature shows. Because in less than six months, she would be handing "her" baby over to Harvey, probably never to be seen again. A wave of sadness suddenly hit her as she thought about it. She was just over a quarter along in the pregnancy and knew what was to come down the line, some of which she was already getting a taste of. Bizarre cravings, intense mood swings, swollen feet, trouble moving around, the list of woes goes on and on. The emotional roller coaster of this whole nine-month journey would probably be the most trying for her, though. But to think that she will have gone through all this hell, not wanting to be pregnant in the first place, just to give the life inside her to someone else, was deeply troubling to her. She foresaw postpartum depression after the delivery.

Suddenly, her phone rang, louder than usual it seemed, snapping her out of these sobering thoughts. It was just the person she wanted calling. Harvey. She rose straight up to pick up her phone off the coffee table.

"Hey Harvey, I'm glad you called me back," she said swiftly, the worry trickling back into her demeanor.

"Yeah, no problem. I got your message. You sounded upset. What's going on?"

"The producers are acting funny and it has me on edge. Why haven't they called or reached out?" Claire's leg started bouncing madly. Any little bit of calmness she gleaned from the nature show was out the window.

"Don't let them get you worked up, Claire. You need to relax for the baby."

"I can't. Not knowing what they're up to is making me go insane."

"Claire, listen to me. You cannot get worked up over them. Neither of us can stress about the unknown. All we can do is hope that whatever they're plotting is in our favor. Okay? Promise me you'll relax."

"Harvey, I can't!" Claire's voice started breaking. "I don't know what they're up to, and I don't want them to do anything that'll upset my baby!" Tears quickly welled up in her eyes and spilled over. An unending stream of tears that had been waiting for their opportunity to fall. Claire had been bottling up insecurities and emotions for a while now, and this was the catalyst to make them come out. "What if they bring back those other hussies you had to choose from to cause trouble for me? You know how they like to bring in drama stirrers."

"Claire, Claire. Don't start thinking that producers are trying to set you up because that'll drive you even more insane. Trust me, I've been there."

"You can never be too sure, though," she cried.

"Claire, I'm coming over there, okay?" Harvey hung up the phone at once.

Claire was left staring at the phone, simultaneously listening to the closing remarks from the nature show narrator.

"...it doesn't matter how big or small the mother is, she will do anything to make sure her babies are out of harm's way." Credits rolled and advertising for the next program immediately came on the screen.

Claire flicked away any remaining tears. She got up and went to the kitchen to make herself some tea. Maybe that could soothe her nerves. She opened the cabinet to practically barren shelves. All she had were two cans of chunky vegetable soup and a box of chamomile that looked six years expired. Better than nothing, she thought.

She took it out and set it on the counter next to the stove as she bent down to retrieve a teapot she had stored in the cupboard below. A nice, antique, ceramic one that was given to her by her mother. It was a family heirloom, dating all the way back to the early 1870s. Claire was admonished by her grandmother and great aunts that if she ever had a daughter, the teapot was to be passed down to her. It was imperative that the practice not be broken. Superstition had it that if the teapot was not passed along to the first subsequent female offspring, the last woman in possession of it would suffer seven years of misfortune in her love life and finances. Claire, being a rational and skeptical thinker, always thought that "curse" was so silly, even to this day. And in retrospect, she realized how selfish the "curse" was too. Anyone who perpetuated the tradition was merely shoving a problem into their child's hands, believing full well that it could bring them years of misery. They were essentially saying, "Here, you deal with it now." Claire seemed to be the only woman in her family with good sense and some kind of moral foundation because she would never knowingly put her child in a potentially harmful situation. In a way, being only a surrogate mother brought a little comfort to her because she didn't have the burden of continuing such a crazy custom, even if she didn't believe in it. Hopefully, she wouldn't even have a girl and then it wouldn't be a concern altogether.

Suddenly, there was a knock on the door. That was fast, Claire thought. She placed the teapot on top of the stove and jogged to the door, looking through the peephole just to be sure it was Harvey. What she saw was a distorted, fisheye view of blond, slicked back hair, but she couldn't see his face. Just the top of his head. She knew it was Harvey, though. While she unfastened the multiple latches and locks, he knocked again, but louder this time.

“Okay! Hold on a minute!” she yelled through the door. When she finally got it open, she gave Harvey an icy look. “I *know* you heard me scrambling to unlock this door. You didn’t have to knock again,” she said bitingly.

“Well hello to you, too!” Harvey replied sarcastically. “I didn’t know it took that long to unlock your own door.”

“You know they secure us in here like we’re supermax inmates,” she joked back. “You came before I was even able to boil some water for some tea. How’d you get here so fast? You fly?”

Harvey laughed. “No, I was actually right down the street at the Whole Foods market. And I just so happened to get your message when I was shopping for kale.” They both giggled over that.

“So you have groceries waiting for you in the car?” Claire asked, heading back into the kitchen.

“Yeah, but just a few things.”

“If you have perishables, those need to get put away ASAP. That’s how it goes.”

“They'll be fine. They won't be in the car for too long.”

“So you don't plan on staying that long? Fine, leave then,” Claire scoffed.

Harvey chuckled lightly. “Well I just came to check on you. I didn't know you wanted me over for a pow-wow.”

“I just expected you to stay a little longer, that's all. I didn't know you were just gonna come and go,” Claire admitted, filling her cursed heirloom with water from the tap.

“You want me to stay, Claire?” She swiveled around to look at Harvey, as he peered over his glasses and furrowed his eyebrows. That did something to her. She grabbed the back of her head and looked away coyly.

She didn't know how to respond. There was a side-busting urge to scream yes, but she didn't want to come off desperate. So instead, her mouth moved around clumsily, groping for something calm to say. “I-if you're not busy or anything, it'd be nice if we could just sit and talk.”

Harvey shoved his hands in his pockets and looked at her intensely. “Sure, we can do that.” His stark blue eyes glued themselves to her. They were reading her. "You seem a lot better from when we were on the phone, by the way."

"Mood swings. What can I say," she said awkwardly, putting the teapot on top of the burner. She turned the dial and up raised a circle of blue flames, crackling three times to indicate that they were in full effect.

"Yeah, mood swings." He continued to stare into her being. There was a discomforting silence to accompany it.

"Hey, did you wanna put your groceries in my fridge?" Claire offered.

"Yeah, that'd be great actually. Thanks. I'll be right back," Harvey said. He left out the apartment to go get his items.

"Okay," Claire replied, tending back to her tea. Hopefully it would be almost done by the time he got back.

As she waited for the water to boil, she thought about the conversation she had with her mom a few days ago at Bev's. A lot of what her mother said was weighing heavy on her mind and got her to really evaluate her feelings. Geraldine was right though. Claire had a special type of something for Harvey, and it was nothing to be ashamed about. She needed to come to terms with how she felt and stop trying to suppress her feelings.

Someone kicked the door to get her attention, rudely interrupting her thoughts. She walked over to the door tensely, wondering who could be obnoxious enough to do such a thing. She peeked through the peephole and, this time, saw Harvey's sharp, long, dimpled nose staring back at her, fibrous nose hairs, cavernous nostrils and all.

When she opened the door and let him in, she realized why he used his foot to knock instead of his hand. He was carrying two big paper bags of groceries. Claire wasn't expecting him to be hauling back what seemed like a lot of stuff. There were green leaves flopping all over the sides of the bag.

"Where can I set these groceries in your fridge?" he asked.

Claire opened her refrigerator door and scanned up and down for a nice spot. For the most part, a lot of the items in her fridge were scattered and unnecessarily placed. So she moved some things around to make room for Harvey's stuff.

"I guess you can put it right here on the bottom shelf," she said.

"Cool. Okay." Harvey set the bags down on the counter and began taking stuff out. First, a cup of organic fig yogurt, then a bottle of extra virgin olive oil. Claire stopped him right there.

"Hey, how much stuff do you have? Looks like you got quite a bit of loose items," she noticed.

"Yeah, I kinda do," Harvey realized.

"Why don't we just put the bags in there as they are instead of taking stuff out? 'Cause then it'll be hell trying to put everything back," Claire suggested. She peeked into both bags and saw just how much he had. "Yeah, I don't feel like putting all this back." She put the yogurt and olive oil back in the bag.

"Fair enough," Harvey conceded. "Tea almost ready?"

"Who said you could have some of my tea?" Claire asked jokingly, picking up both bags to put them in the fridge. They were heavier than she thought. She struggled a little, but managed to hold on to them. "Nah, I don't need no help," she said to Harvey with sarcasm.

"Oh! I'm sorry!" He immediately rushed to her aid, taking a bag off her hands. "Where is my head at right now?"

Claire opened her mouth, getting ready to say something but relented. "You don't even wanna know what just popped into my head."

Harvey looked at her confused. "What?" She didn't answer. "What?" he asked louder.

"Never mind. I just need to get my mind out the gutter right now."

Harvey contorted his face in confusion. He still wasn't catching on. Claire looked at him as if to say, "Really think about what you just said, and connect the dots." Then the realization slowly dawned on him. "Oh—Claire, how could you!"

"How could I what?" she asked, trying to act innocent. Steam finally came out the teapot. She turned the burner off and took the teapot off the stove.

"How could you think like that? I thought you were a classy, mature lady," Harvey said.

"I am. I think I'm just sexually frustrated and my mind is…leaning in that direction."

"When's the last time you, ya know, made love to somebody?" Harvey wanted to know.

"Daaaang. Nosy much?" Claire poked.

"Just curious, is all. I thought we were comfortable enough with each other to discuss stuff like this."

"I mean, this topic is a little touchy for me," she told him. "It's been a very long time since I got any."

"How far back, though? College? High school?"

"You really wanna know, don't you? Wow. I've never met someone so persistent about another person's sex life. That's kinda weird."

They both laughed. Claire grabbed two mugs from the cupboard. She figured she might as well be hospitable to Harvey. He did drop what he was doing to come and check on her, after all. He didn't have to do that.

"You want chamomile? That's what I'm making for myself," Claire said.

"Sure, that sounds good." Harvey got comfortable and took off his leather jacket, gently setting it on the back of a chair in the dining area. He took a seat and waited patiently for his cup.

Claire poured the scalding hot water into both mugs, nabbed two teabags from the box, and dropped them in. "You know, you don't really strike me as a tea drinker. You seem more like a coffee guy."

"I am actually. But I will dabble into tea on occasion. It centers me," he said, his cheesy attempt to sound cultured and spiritual.

"It centers you? Oh, okay, Mr. Harvey. Where'd that even come from?" Claire laughed, bringing him his tea. "Hope it's not too stale for ya," she joked.

"Stale? Ha ha." He blew on it a few times and then took a very slight sip. He smacked his lips to get the flavor working in his mouth. "Not bad. Why'd you say stale?"

"Oh, I don't know. It just looked like it had been sitting in my cabinet for God knows how long," she replied.

"Oh." Harvey chuckled, taking another shallow sip. "So there's this elephant in the room that I *know* you know is here."

Claire's eyes instantly darted to the corner. She had no clue what he was talking about. "I don't feel any elephants. What, are you talking about that dirty joke I almost made?"

"No, Claire." Harvey was a little frustrated that she was oblivious. "The elephant is when I told you I love you and you went silent and hung up on me."

"Ohhh," she whispered guiltily. "Wait. Is that why you came here? Just to tell me that? Did you come here just to make me feel bad?" Hormones were kicking in again.

"No. No. Claire, I genuinely came by to make sure you were alright. But we can't sit around and ignore what happened. That was a pretty big deal. But I need to know... if...the feeling is mutual."

Claire stared into her cup of tea trying to avoid eye contact with him. Now was her moment to lay her feelings on the table. No better opportunity could've presented itself. "Harvey, umm—"

Suddenly, Harvey's phone rang. In a way, Claire was relieved, but at the same time, disappointed, because now *would've* been the best chance to come clean about her true feelings for him.

"Hello?" Harvey answered.

"Hey Harv, this is Stan."

"Harv?" Harvey mouthed to himself. Stan had never called him that before, and it was mighty strange that he started doing it now. Another addition to the list of weird that production was showing.

"The other producers and I reviewed you and Claire's applications, green screen interviews, you know all that preliminary junk? And effective next week, there's gonna be some interesting changes. We've really been deliberating on some things and uh…we think it'll bring some pizzazz to the show. That's why you haven't heard from us in a while. But trust us, it'll be very interesting."

Stan made sure that he relayed the most vague and cryptic message he could. Nothing he said was false, but it also wasn't the entire truth. The truth of the matter was the producers were trying to stir up drama. They had been sifting through hours of footage of one-on-one sessions with Claire and Harvey, as well as written questionnaire responses. All in a concerted effort to find any type of dirt to use on them in the coming months of filming. They needed something—or someone—to spice up the show. And it looks like they had finally found what they were looking for.

Chapter 7

As Claire was being mic'ed by a production assistant, she couldn't shake the feeling that something weird was about to happen. Everyone on the crew had been acting strange since they had convened on "set." Stan, Brent, the cameramen, the sound guys, they were all in on a secret and Claire was anxious to know what it was. The uncertainty of the whole situation had her on edge, to say the least. Not even the gorgeous view of the marina nor the beautiful flora surrounding them could rein in her nerves. Today, they were filming at a very elegant rooftop bistro overlooking a river near Sherman Oaks. The high class restaurant was appropriately named "Bourgeois."

The purpose of today's scene was to have Claire and Harvey discuss names for the baby, hopefully opening up a conversation that would reveal more of their pasts. This was in an effort to include a more substantial storyline and not just have flat, one-layered characters. But Claire had a hunch that the scene would not turn out anywhere near what it was supposed to. She just knew for a fact that a monkey wrench would be thrown into the mix somehow. She and Harvey exchanged dubious looks, almost like they were communicating telepathically. Neither of them had said a word since they had shown up to the taping.

The PA did a final wire check before she ran out of sight. Claire looked around confused, wondering where she had disappeared to. Stan noticed this and came over to give her and Harvey a pep talk before filming commenced. He was intentionally trying to distract her from what was really going on.

"You guys ready for this?" Stan asked, clapping his hands together.

"Ready as we'll ever be," Claire retorted, looking broodingly at Harvey. Harvey didn't say a word. His apprehension about what was to come was expressed through utter silence.

"Hey, that's good enough for me, Claire," Stan replied, playfully smacking her on the shoulder with the back of his hand.

She turned her face away from him rolling her eyes. Then she noticed in her peripheral vision three big, muscular dudes posted at the far end of the rooftop. This caught her attention, causing her to swing her head back in Stan's direction. "Who are those guys?" she asked, frowning with bewilderment.

"Let's just say they're here for physical reinforcement in case things get out of hand," he answered, giving Claire a sneaky wink, and taking his position behind the main camera.

This, of course, made her more uneasy than she already was. These guys looked like straight up bodyguards and there had never been a need for them before, so why was this any different? Claire knew without a doubt that something was about to go down. And she had no idea what tricks were in store for her. Her adrenaline started going, causing her leg to shake madly.

"Claire, you alright?" Harvey asked stupidly.

"Does it seem like I'm alright?" she kind of snapped. She leaned in and drastically lowered her voice so none of the producers or crew would hear her. "Did you catch what he just said? He said they're here for physical reinforcement. That's red flag number one. Why do you need these bouncer dudes when we're just supposed to be talking about baby names?"

“Places, people!” a producer yelled. Everyone scurried to their respective jobs. Harvey wanted to give Claire his opinion, but it was too late. It was time to start. He didn’t know what else to do besides shrug at her and pretend like this whole thing was just beyond him.

Stan held up his hand and began counting down from five on his fingers. Then he pointed, and it was show time. Two camera guys were posted on either side of the table and were aiming their lenses exceptionally close to Claire and Harvey’s faces. There was a reason they were trying to get close-ups. They needed to capture every emotion and facial quirk they could, down to the slightest nerve twitch. Claire just knew they were going to chop and screw the footage horribly to fit their agenda, to make the scene much more dramatic than it actually plays out. That’s why they needed as many clips to work with as possible, so they could pull from whatever, to totally manipulate reaction shots. Whatever they would do to spice up the scene, there was no doubt that it was going to be very intense.

“I’m glad you were able to meet with me for lunch today, Claire,” Harvey said, kicking the scene off the way it was planned.

"Oh, yeah, absolutely. I had some free time, so I figured I'd come down," she said, taking a sip of water.

"How have you been since the last time I saw you?" Harvey leaned back in his chair and hoisted his elbow up onto the edge of its back.

"Not bad, not bad," Claire replied. She wasn't really pressed for the small talk. She was just ready for whatever the producers had schemed up to happen already. *Let's cut the pleasantries and get to it,* she thought. Although, at least the conversation they were having on camera wasn't rehearsed. Not that the others were, but prior to this taping session, Stan was notorious for steering the conversation instead of the people who actually had to have it.

"Has the baby been giving you any trouble?" Harvey asked.

"Aside from making me crave watermelon drizzled with Italian dressing or corn chips crushed up and mixed in with yogurt? Not much," she joked. Harvey let out a hardy chuckle. "These hormones have my emotions running the gamut, though. I'll say that much."

Harvey blew a huge gust of wind out of his mouth. "I can't even imagine what that's like." He reached for his glass of water, taking off the lemon wedge and squeezing a few drops of juice into it. He gently swirled his drink, watching the ice cubes carousel around the cup. "This is why I'm glad *you're* the one who has to carry."

"Ha ha. Very funny," Claire replied dryly. "Geez, if only we were seahorses. It'd be a whole different ball game, buddy."

"Seahorses? What're you talking about?" Harvey was genuinely confounded.

"What am I *talking* about?" Claire rose up a little in her seat, surprised that her comment went right over his head. Harvey struck her as way smarter than what he just displayed, so she was shocked. "You mean to tell me you've never heard of female seahorses transferring the babies over to the father after she carries them for so long? That's like common knowledge."

"Claire, I know about a lot of things, but that ain't one of 'em."

She stared back at him with the most dumbfounded expression. “Have you been living under a rock for thirty years? ‘Cause oh my gosh. I think even five-year-olds know that,” she teased.

“Oh, for real?”

“Yes, seriously. You should’ve learned that in like third grade, bro. I’m honestly kinda glad that this baby inside of me isn’t yours, because if it was…it would have a hard time in school.”

“Claire, I cannot stand you.” Harvey couldn’t help but laugh because it was sincerely funny. Even if it was at his expense. “But I don’t like us calling the baby an ‘it.’ When are we gonna find out the sex?”

“What’s this, July? So around mid-August, we should go and see what the sex is. I’ll be at least 18 weeks pregnant by then.”

“Yes, that’d be great. ‘Cause we need to start brainstorming names for the little one.”

"For the heck of it, let's just throw out some common unisex names, any ones you can think of," Claire suggested.

"Okay, sounds like fun." He swallowed. "Okay, um… Riley?"

"Riley is cool. Especially if the baby's a little fireball, that would be perfect. What about Alex or Taylor?"

"Can you really consider Alex unisex, though?"

"Well yeah, kinda. The nickname is, at least. But we obviously know if it's a girl, she'll be Alexandria and if it's a boy, he'll be Alexander."

"True, true. Uh...how 'bout Micah? Or Linsey? Or Blake?"

"Those are all really good too. But none of these are really hitting. There's gotta be some unisex name out there that's sorta common, but unique at the same time. Something with pop to it."

"Terry?" Harvey asked.

"Nah, Terry's kinda boring. I was thinking Blaise."

"Blaise is a rad name. But I think we should name the baby that only if it ends up being born under a fire sign," Harvey recommended, giving Claire a corny wink.

"Well, I'm not sure how that's gonna work because my expected due date is like late January. So it'll more than likely end up being a Capricorn or an Aquarius. Maybe even a Pisces if it refuses to come out on time."

"None of those are fire signs?" Harvey asked yet another dumb question.

Claire stared so hard and long at him. "Harvey. Really think about those zodiac signs. Pisces is a fish. That's water. Aquarius sounds like it's water, but it's actually air, I think. And Capricorn is like a goat with a fishtail or something like that? But I think it's an earth sign if I'm not mistaken. So no, none of those are fire, Harvey. The closest fire sign that the baby could be born under is Sagittarius, but he or she would have to be a preemie," she explained.

"Hmm, interesting," Harvey said, feigning intrigue. "What are you, by the way?"

“I’m a Scorpio,” she answered, purposely giving him the stereotypical penetrating look that her zodiac sign was known for.

“Really? I never would’ve guessed that. I’m an Aries. Aries is an air sign, right?”

Claire closed her eyes and chuckled loudly, in sheer disbelief that he could be so clueless.

“What?” Harvey asked, getting agitated. “Isn’t that why they call it Air-reez? Because it’s an air sign?”

Claire pinched the bridge of her nose. “No, Harvey. Aries is a fire sign. Just like Sagittarius.”

“Ohhhh, okay. That explains why my mom always told me I was born a hothead. ‘Cause neither of my parents were fussy like me. So that makes sense.”

“You’ve never read a description of your sign in like newspapers and magazines? Aries people have very short fuses. That’s nothing new. That’s like one of you guys’ top three traits. You know what’s interesting, though? Both of our star signs are governed by the same planet, which is Mars. It’s supposed to represent aggression, and violence, and sex drive."

"I guess that's where Scorpios get their freakiness from. If I don't know anything else about astrology, I do know that Scorpios are like gods in the bedroom."

Claire smirked shyly. "Yeah, we're pretty racy."

"That's an understatement, girl. But what I don't get about Scorpios is why they think they're so bad. I mean, they literally walk around like everyone is supposed to fear them or something. Why, just 'cause you guys have poisonous stingers?"

"We do not walk around like that," Claire rebutted, sounding genuinely offended. "If anything, it's Aries folks who throw their weight around and act super domineering. You guys *have* to command *everything*. It's so annoying."

"*I'm* not like that, though. But seriously, Scorps aren't the most fun folk to be around. You guys have really heavy, dark energy a lot of times. From how you look at people, to the vibes you guys give off—"

"Aww, do we scare you?" Claire teased.

"You guys don't scare me, because I'm an Aries, remember? We're like the most courageous sign, I *do* know that. We charge anything and anyone head on. That's why our symbol is the ram. But I just feel like Scorpios try too hard to be intimidating and edgy."

"Don't forget emotionally volatile and vindictive," a female voice interjected out of nowhere. Claire and Harvey whipped their heads around to see where the voice came from.

The camera guy who was standing nearest to Claire got even closer to her face than before. Her jaw dropped once she realized who it was. Harvey, on the other hand, was every bit of puzzled. He didn't know who this girl was and why she was here. A third camera guy, who seemed to magically appear from a trapdoor, stationed himself right at the entrance to the rooftop where she was walking from.

This girl was someone with a bold presence and striking look, someone made for the cameras. Smooth, milk chocolate skin with long, wavy hair extensions, a huge rack, and perfectly sized butt. Her gaudy jewelry jangled and clanked as she walked; from the obnoxiously large triangle earrings in her ears to the millions of metallic bangles and bracelets that shined too brilliantly for human eyes. Her face was smothered in makeup, but it somehow didn't look overdone. The hot pink lip gloss, fake eyelashes, and glittery eye shadow were applied somewhat tastefully. What she was wearing was kind of kitschy, though—a neon green mesh shawl draped over a bright yellow lace tunic that barely came down pass her knees. And one would not be wrong in assuming that she wasn't wearing underwear. She strutted towards the table in her obviously fake designer pumps, which totally clashed with the general color scheme she had going on with the rest of her wardrobe.

"That's why Libras are better," she said snootily, laughing at herself. Claire rolled her eyes so hard, the whites of her eyeballs fluttered vigorously. "Hey, big sis! How are you?"

Claire gave her sister the iciest glare. "Hello, Mercedes. Long time, no see," she replied coldly.

The third camera guy followed Mercedes to the table, sidestepping to get an angle of her from the front. She was donning the widest grin, intentionally flashing her snow white teeth. She noticed Harvey, and immediately went to shake his hand, a little bit too affectionately for Claire's taste.

"Hi! I'm Mercedes! Nice to meet you!" she said, covering his hand with her other hand.

"Hi! I'm Harvey. Pleasure's all mine," he said, his eyes twinkling at the sight of this young beauty. Claire caught this and didn't know if he was smitten by her or just blinded by her dazzling accessories. There was a moment of sheer silence and discomfort. Claire's Scorpio eyes continued glaring venomously at her little sister. Harvey felt the tension and cleared his throat to break it.

"H-have a seat," he stammered. "Please."

"Thanks!" Mercedes glanced nervously back and forth between Claire and Harvey, not knowing what to expect herself. She set her purple leather clutch on the table, and then sat.

"So you two are sisters?" Harvey asked, still in amazement.

"Yeah, I'm her baby sister. We're six years apart." A tall waiter suddenly came to the table with a glass of water for Mercedes. She looked up at him, mouthing her thanks.

"Claire, you didn't tell me you had a sister," Harvey said, looking at her as if he wanted her to explain herself.

"That's because I don't," she retorted flatly.

The tension grew even thicker. Mercedes looked down at the ground, not knowing what to say. "Um…well clearly, that's not entirely true since she's sitting right here," Harvey replied slowly, careful so as not to rile her up with any wrong word.

Claire sat up and leaned forward toward him. "No, you don't get it. Any *sister* I once had has been nonexistent for about four years now, so…" She sat back in her seat and rocked slightly, trying to restrain herself from lashing out at Mercedes. There was evidently some really bad blood between them.

Claire was so direct and callous that the stillness following each one of her statements became increasingly uncomfortable. And these were long periods of quiet, too.

Harvey was especially surprised that Stan hadn't stepped in by now to push the scene along.

Mercedes finally found the courage to speak up. "Claire, I came here to make peace. I don't want there to be any awkwardness between us."

Claire turned to look at the producers. "Why are you guys letting her talk to me? Why is she even here? Get this trash outta my face."

"Okay now, Claire. You're taking it a little bit too far, now. She hasn't done anything to you. Be nice." Harvey was getting visibly frustrated. Until Claire provided a valid reason as to why she was being so nasty towards her sister, he saw no justification for her acting like this.

"Harvey, you don't know anything about me or Mercedes, so just don't speak, okay?"

"No! I feel like you're bullying her when she hasn't done anything to you!"

“Bullying?” Claire chuckled. “Mercedes, tell him how much of a skank you are, and why we haven’t spoken in four years.”

Mercedes had enough of the insults. “Okay, you know what, I tried to be cordial with you, but I see you wanna take it there.” She fumbled with her earring like she was getting ready to take it off. Then she looked at Stan. “You guys didn’t tell me she was gonna be this catty.”

“Girl, stop lying. You know good and well you didn’t come here to make peace and be cool with me. You just came to irritate my life once again, and try to take what’s mine.”

Harvey frowned. He had no idea what Claire was getting at. “What do you mean ‘take what’s yours?’”

“My little sister’s a bona fide slut. Four years ago, when she was only eighteen, she stole my boyfriend, someone who I really loved and was talking about spending the rest of my life with. She waltzed her little hot self into the picture and ruined my relationship. She’s a homewrecker.”

“Lies. He didn’t really want you, Claire. You were delusional.” Mercedes took off her other earring.

"No, I'm not. You better watch who you're talking to, because I will drag you all up and through this town," she snapped. "Over my dead body will you try to flirt with Harvey and get with him. Him and *I* are a thing, not him and *you*." Harvey jerked his head back in astonishment. He couldn't believe that Claire, out of her own mouth, said they were an item.

"Insecure much? Honey, if I wanted to flirt with Harvey, you would know, believe that. I definitely wasn't flirting."

"Oh, that's right. Libras are like extra friendly and that often gets misperceived as flirtatiousness. I forgot. Those darn Libras," she came back mockingly.

"Well those darn Libras are the very ones who can take ya man so flawlessly because we're just the most beautiful things to grace this planet," Mercedes clapped back. "If I wanted your Harvey, I could have him," she continued in such a comported but firm tone.

Apparently, production felt the heat intensifying between the two and anticipated a physical altercation because one of the security personnel stood right at the table. But that's exactly what they wanted. This was the scene they had been plotting for the whole time. And if they threw clips of this fight in the trailer and teasers, it would be sure to garner lots of viewership.

"Sweetheart, you could never in a *billion* years have Harvey. He would never want something as tacky as you," Claire replied angrily.

"Don't call me sweetheart, because I'm not your sweetheart," Mercedes told her, thrusting her hand towards Claire's face.

"Okay, Mercedes, you *know* I don't take too kindly to people putting their hands in my face. So I advise you to reel that back in before you get popped in the face."

Mercedes stood up, just as the security guard stepped beside her and blocked her with his arm. Claire remained sitting, unfazed but ready to go if it came down to it.

"Mercedes, who are you trying to scare? I will slap you so hard, every single one of those big, white Chiclets in your mouth will be scattered all over this roof. Every single one of them."

In the blink of an eye, Mercedes grabbed her glass of water and chucked it at Claire. It barely missed her face by an inch or two, making a loud crash as it shattered against the ground. Water did manage to splash the side of Claire's face, though, causing her to flip her lid. Security pulled Mercedes back from the table. Claire impulsively grabbed the first thing at her disposal, which was a bundle of silverware and launched them toward Mercedes' head.

"Hey! Hey! Hey!" Harvey yelled, flying out of his seat and stepping in between them.

"DON'T YOU EVER THROW A DRINK AT ME, YOU LITTLE—" Claire was so livid, she couldn't even finish her sentence. She threw herself forward and grabbed a large clump of Mercedes hair, punching the top of her head like crazy. She landed at least five good hits before Harvey wrapped his arm around her stomach and yoked her away from her sister. She was screaming out expletives and threatening to quit the show if they didn't remove Mercedes from the premises.

The other two security guards, by this time, were now involved, trying to disconnect the two of them before they inflicted more damage. Claire was tightly gripping Mercedes' hair while Mercedes refused to let go of Claire's shirt. Stan ran over yelling for both of them to let go. It was such a mess that even one of the camera guys had to stop filming to help break up the melee. After almost ten minutes of that very intense struggle, they both eventually let go.

"Aha! You couldn't even cause me bodily harm 'cause you're so weak!" Claire shouted.

"I could've grabbed your hair, but you don't have any, so there's that!"

"Exactly. My baldness came in handy today, right? I bet you're mad, right? Remember all those times when you would make fun of me for cutting off all my hair when we were teenagers? And that's all you know how to do is pull hair. Even before I cut off my hair, you used to go straight for the hair when we would fight as kids. I hate you. Why are you even my sister?"

Chapter 8

"I just want you to know that I don't blame you for reacting how you did last week with Mercedes. After you explained to me how spiteful and conniving she can be, I realized, yeah, your feelings were *definitely* warranted that day," Harvey said, chuckling a little. "I think any normal person who had a sister like her would react the same way."

"She just really annoys my spirit, Harvey. That girl's had it out for me since we were *kids*! And she has not let up since!" Claire cradled her glass of cranberry juice, staring at it as if it was the drink she was upset with.

Harvey threw back his second shot of tequila, slamming the glass down on the counter. He grunted as the alcohol scalded his chest, but knew that it was certainly needed. Once the burning subsided, he turned to her seriously. "Did you really mean that, though? When you said you hate her and that you wish she was never your sister?" Claire looked to the side sheepishly. "Because that was kinda harsh. I was like 'whoa.'"

"Harvey…I really meant that." She paused to look straight into his eyes, to let him know that she was absolutely *not* joking. "I really cannot stand her to the point where I don't even know why we share the same DNA." She took a swig of drink and let it sit in her mouth for a bit before she swallowed. "She's the one person in this world that can get under my skin like no other human can."

Harvey shook his head. "The producers are super shady. They knew exactly what they were doing when they brought her on."

"Yeah, but it's their job. Can't really fault them for that," Claire defended, taking a sip of her drink while she stared off contemplatively. Harvey's eyes widened. He was shocked that she actually vouched for them. "It's not their duty to be concerned about the feelings of the cast members. Their goal is to get ratings and make money, and they're gonna do that any way they can."

Harvey was confused. She seemed to be preaching the exact opposite of what she argued with Stan about a couple of months ago.

"But Claire, what happened to ethics? You don't treat people like that, regardless of what your *job* is. Weren't you the same person on a soapbox about the exploitation of reality TV?"

Claire drowsily rolled her eyes at Harvey. "At the end of the day, I don't care. What's done is done. As long as they don't bring her around again, I'm cool."

"If they did, what would you do?"

"Are you kidding me? I'd stomp that skank into the ground and not think twice about it. She crossed the line throwing a drink in my face. You better hope I don't *ever* film with her again."

"Claire—"

"No, I'm serious, Harvey. My sister and I have had many fights, but never to this magnitude. She *really* messed up this time. When I see her, it's war. If someone as much as mention her name, I'm goin' off. Bet on it."

"Claire, no. You're better than that. You're classy and poised. This is not you."

"I. Hate. Her. Do you not grasp that concept? I hate her!" Claire was easing into a raging lunatic. Her eyes slightly danced around and she was starting to slur her words.

"Listen, I know you're upset that Stan fined you, but you just gotta suck it up and deal. I mean, you *had* to know that there were gonna be consequences for you bopping Mercedes' head like you were trying to get Mario coins or something."

"Seriously? So corny what you just said." Claire shook her head and put it down on the table like she was about to take a nap.

"What? You were! And the look on your face while you were doing it was scary! I never wanna see you like that again."

Claire grumbled something indistinct, her head still buried in her arms. Harvey flagged down the bartender and asked him for a water.

"Claire, you resume filming in a week. We need to get you together before then."

She grumbled again. The bartender came back with a water. Harvey nodded in appreciation for it and gently shook Claire.

“Claire, come on. I have some water for you to drink. You just gotta drink, c’mon.”

She finally rose up, her eyelids half open. He held the glass up to her mouth as she took in sharp gulps. “That’s it, Claire. Drink some more.” She guzzled a few more times and stopped.

“Thanks for being here for me, Harvey.” Her tone had done a complete 180.

“It’s no problem. I’m always here for you.” Harvey rubbed her shoulder, and signaled for the bartender to get her another water.

“You’re truly an amazing guy. I just want you to know that. And…thanks for stepping in when my sister and I fought. Even though it took like thirty production crew members to pry us apart. I know that was crazy. I should apologize to you for putting you in that predicament.”

“Listen, I totally understand where that emotion came from. Could you have handled the situation better? Yes. I don’t think she ever would’ve thrown the drink at you had you not been making digs at her the moment she stepped onto the scene. I think if you had just played it cool until she got gully with you first, then your blow up would’ve been more justified. But *she* was the one that turned it physical, not you.”

“I wonder if the producers told her to do that, ya know? I wouldn’t be surprised.”

“I wouldn’t put it past them. They were devious enough to bring her on, why not take it the extra mile by playing her against you?”

“True.” The bartender returned with a second water. “Thanks, guy.” She inserted her straw from her other drink into that one. “If it wasn’t for my transparency, they probably wouldn’t have known she existed, though.”

“What d’you mean?”

“Well, you know, during the audition process, when they ask you about past relationships and people you don’t get along with, and blah, blah, blah? Yeah, my sister’s name came up, and I was not shy in telling them all about her. Should've known they were gonna use this information against me at some point. They ask you about dirt like that for a reason."

"Yeah, but that's how they do everybody. Don't feel bad because they did me the exact same way when I filmed that Billion-Heirs show. Producers have to do that, though. It's like protocol for any reality show."

"They asked me some very intrusive questions, too. I didn't too much like that," Claire said, putting herself back in that moment.

"Oh yeah, they'll get all up in your business. That's unavoidable."

"Hey, can I ask you something?" Claire peered into Harvey's eyes with sincerity.

"Sure, anything."

"Do you think any less of me after what happened with Mercedes?"

There was a long pause. Harvey took in a breath and held Claire's hand. "Claire, I thought it'd be clear that my feelings toward you have not changed. I don't think any less of you. I still think you're an amazing woman, strong, independent, and classy. You just had a bad moment. Don't let this diminish your character."

"Thank you," she said, her eyes tearing up slightly.

"Just use this as a mirror to reflect on how *not* to react next time." Still grasping her hand, he leaned in to kiss her on the cheek. It was the sweetest gesture he had done to her. The moment his lips touched her face, it's like her entire body floated upward while she was still planted on the bar stool. During his kiss, she smelled his cologne, light and masculine, enveloping her senses. She felt like she was slowly ascending to nirvana.

*****

In a weird way, Claire was glad to be back to filming. She didn't think she'd ever feel like that either. The feeling was almost kind of like being suspended from school and finally returning after so many days, thinking that you'd hate it, but you end up realizing how much you really missed it. Stan had placed her on “temporary leave,” basically a timeout so she could think about what she had done. Plus, he figured she would be a liability due to her “volatile behavior” and thought it would be best for her to take a breather to get herself together. And just to ensure that she never lashed out like that again, he imposed a fine on her. $1,500 would be docked from her paycheck.

Now she was back in the saddle, back to the old routine, waiting for the cameras to start rolling for her one-on-one interview with a producer. She had hoped it wouldn’t be Stan who asked the questions because she was still kind of upset with him for the situation with Mercedes. She knew beyond a doubt that he was the one who orchestrated the whole thing and thought it was dirty for him to penalize her for something *he* set up in the first place.

At any rate, she sat in the makeshift green screen room in her apartment as a production assistant, just outside the door, called Brent to prep himself for Claire’s interview. Claire could breathe now. As long as she didn’t have to see Stan’s face. The PA came in the room to brief Claire on what was about to happen.

“Okay, so Brent’s gonna be conducting your interview. He’s just gonna ask you about your fight with Mercedes and how you feel about it, and blasé blah, okay?”

Claire nodded her agreement. Brent promptly entered with a clipboard of questions and took a seat beside the camera. “You ready, Claire?”

“Ready as I’ll ever be,” she said unexcitedly.

Brent sarcastically gave her a thumbs up and proceeded right into the interrogation. “Alrighty, so first things first. What was it about Mercedes that really got under your skin? What made you be so snippy towards her the moment she showed up?”

Claire looked away to mentally relive those moments leading up to that explosive clash. “Mercedes and I have always had a very turbulent relationship. I’m almost convinced that God gave her to my mother, just so he could test my patience. She’s just an obnoxious individual.”

“Do you regret attacking her the way you did?”

"Well, first of all, she technically attacked me first by throwing a drink at my face. So let's just check that."

"But you don't think you egged her on by being rude to her from the gate?"

"Yeah, I was rude to her, absolutely. But I *don't* regret that because she deserved it. I could've swung on her at first glance if I wanted to, but I tried to control myself. The fact that *she* was the one who turned the altercation physical shows that she's mentally weak, that she doesn't know how to hold her own in a verbal argument. Our mom taught us to use our words, and only resort to blows when it's self-defense. She totally disregarded that. So me being rude to her was no valid excuse to throw a drink at my face."

"What was going through your mind as you pounded her head in?"

Claire chuckled. "My thoughts were to kill this girl. Beat her to where she's unrecognizable. I literally wanted her to die in that moment."

"Wow, that's kinda extreme, don't you think?"

"Well, maybe not die. But I definitely wanted to cause her severe bodily harm. And it wouldn't just be for what she did in the present, but *all* of the foul stuff she's done to me in life. She was gonna learn that day that I was never the one to be trifled with. Not yesterday, not today, not ever."

"Did you at least for one second think about the potential fatality that could've resulted with your baby?" Brent's voice turned personal. You could tell that this question sprung from his own volition, not some pre-drafted questions he was told to ask.

"I honestly didn't, Brent—"

Brent held up his hand. "You can't use my name," he curtly interrupted.

"Sorry. Anyway, as I was saying, I wasn't thinking about the baby when I fought her. That could've turned out so many different ways, and I just thank God that it didn't result in a miscarriage."

"So no damage was inflicted on the baby?" Brent sounded as if he needed closure so as not to be unduly upset with her.

"None, thankfully. I went to the doctor two days after the fight because I was aching so much from being yanked around and manhandled by security and production. The doctor did an ultrasound and said that the baby was fine for the most part. His only concern was that all that jostling around could result in some problems down the line after the baby is born."

"During that doctor visit, I'm sure you found out the sex since the doctor did an ultrasound."

"You know what? I'm glad you said that because actually I opted to *not* know what the sex was. I told the doctor not to tell me. I wanna be genuinely surprised when we film that scene."

"You can't mention that on camera, Claire."

"Oops, sorry. An ultrasound never happened then." She pretended as if she was locking her mouth shut and throwing away the key.

"Back to the debacle between you and Mercedes, explain more about this whole her-stealing-your-boyfriend business. How long were you and your ex together?"

“We were together for at least a year and a half. It was no secret that he was gonna propose to me eventually. I knew it was coming because we had been talking about marriage and kids for a while. Family had no idea about him, though.”

“How did your sister come into the picture then?”

“I had actually been hiding him that whole time from everybody because I didn’t know how they’d receive him. My friends and family were all expecting for me to get with a certain type of guy, and this guy I was dating was literally the exact opposite. I just didn’t want them to scare him off, or convince me that he wasn’t a good fit for me. But when I felt it getting serious, I decided to bring him along to a family function that my grandma was having at her house. I was finally ready to introduce him to my folks. And then Mercedes laid eyes on him, and it was over from there. Once she sinks her teeth into something—or someone—there’s really nothing that can be done.”

“So where did you and your ex’s relationship start to fall apart?”

“Once Mercedes got in his head about me. She was able to sway him into thinking that he’d be better off with a young, seductive vixen like herself who was entering the prime of her life, instead of being with an 'old chick' like me who was almost five years shy of thirty. He fell for it, and ended up leaving me for her."

"How was the split?"

"It was more sad than anything. I wasn't necessarily angry with him. Because he sat me down and told me in a very nice way that he would much rather prefer someone a little closer to his age—he was twenty at the time—and I understood that. But at the same time, it was still like a very abrupt gut punch, ya know? Like we're perfect for each other. Look what we've built together. Why do we have to end things like this?"

Brent paused. The duplicitous look on his face made Claire feel like he was about to ask something she wouldn't like. "Do you think that if given the opportunity, Mercedes would try something like this again?"

The question was almost as forceful as the gut punch she experienced when her ex-boyfriend told her he was leaving her. "Let's not even entertain that thought."

"Fair enough. Hey, could you hang out for a sec? I need to use the bathroom right quick."

"Sure." Brent got up to go "relieve himself."

As Claire sat patiently waiting, twiddling her thumbs, she noticed the monitor beside the camera suddenly turn on. It was weird because it had been off the whole time she was interviewing with Brent. Immediately, Claire got wary. Of course the screen would conveniently come on as soon as a producer leaves the room.

The screen was blue for about ten seconds with a timer going at the bottom. Then a picture glitched in, which looked like really rough surveillance footage. The numbers were still counting at the bottom. There were two people sitting in a bar, a man and a woman, laughing and talking with each other. At first, Claire couldn't make out who they were. But then as she focused in on their faces, she realized that they were none other than Harvey and her sister, Mercedes. Claire's insides turned completely cold, but her face turned completely hot. She felt intensely empty and angered at the same time. In a split second, her entire feelings for Harvey inverted. She just knew something was going on between them two but didn't know to what extent.

What if they had been spending time together behind her back, long before Mercedes even made her appearance on the show? What if Harvey and Mercedes were in cahoots, working together to make Claire look like a fool? What if Harvey and Mercedes had been dating each other for a while, well before this show even existed, and this was all just an elaborate hoax? Claire's suspicions were plausible, but they were also fueled by her vacillating hormones. It was abundantly clear that Brent left out the room for another reason than he let on. He and the other producers purposely "leaked" that footage to stir Claire up and rouse her paranoia. And it worked.

Her first thought was to storm out the room and brazenly declare her withdrawal from the show. But then she didn't want to give them the satisfaction of getting to her. So instead she got up to position the camera the way she wanted it and sat poised, staring directly into the lens.

"Hi Brent, Stan, Trish. I wanna thank you guys so much for not leaving me in the dark about Harvey and Mercedes.

Thank you for not making me look stupid on national TV. But I hereby quit the show. I want my contract terminated and I would like for the cameras to not follow me anymore. And most importantly, I want this pregnancy over so that I can hand this baby over to Harvey and not have anything to do with him ever again. Oh, and I still need to get paid. Yes, honey. I still need my coins. I didn't get impregnated and put my life on blast for the world to see for *free*. Make the check payable to Claire Rexall. And honestly, I should get a raise for all the hell I've been through on this show. If you guys don't honor that, I could always resort to suing you for emotional damages and putting my life in danger by having guest stars toss glasses at my *face*. Last request is to receive a check for at least a thousand every time an episode airs on TV, including reruns, in addition to teasers, promos, and trailers that are released that feature *me* in them. Thank you guys. Muah!" She blew a kiss to the camera and snatched off her mic, ripping a wire in the process.

As she made her way to the door, Trish stepped from out of nowhere to diffuse her. "Claire, let's talk about this. We —"

"What's there to talk about? I'm done with this show. I feel like all of you guys were in on this sham to make me look like an idiot. I thought I'd finally met someone I could connect with, but he's just like every other guy. More into my sister than me."

Chapter 9

Claire's face was crawling with fury as she sat in Stan's office, her arms folded tightly. The scariest part of her expression had to be her vengeful Scorpio eyes. There was nothing like the venomous, death-dealing glare of a human scorpion. And unfortunately, Harvey was on the receiving end of that terrifying stare. His Aries toughness was no match for the small, but powerful arachnid. Her eyes cut deep into his psyche.

"Claire, I promise you, it's not what you think," he said remorsefully. "Stan's gonna explain everything to you.

Claire said absolutely nothing. Her silence was so freezing cold that it permeated the entire room, reaching down into the depths of Harvey's bones. He could feel ice coursing through his veins. It would take *a lot* of convincing for him to get back in her good graces.

Stan entered the room looking slightly irritated. He looked as though he did not want to be bothered with either of them. Taking a seat in his black leather chair, he glanced at

Harvey waiting for him to speak first since he was the one who called the meeting.

"Stan, could you please tell Claire what the deal was?"

"What're you talking about?" Stan frowned.

"Oh, now you wanna act clueless. Come on, Stan. We already know you guys intentionally showed Claire a clip of me and Mercedes together at Rory's. Where *nothing* happened between her and I."

"You guys were giggling and chatting with each other so comfortably," Claire finally spoke up. "I saw her feeling on your arm and nuzzling her nose up against your cheek. There's no way you can tell me that was just a friendly encounter."

"Claire, her being extra touchy with me doesn't mean anything's going on between us. You gotta stop being so paranoid."

"No, *I* know my sister. And I know that if you allow her to get *that* close to you, something else is sure to follow. She's a succubus. And you fell for her tricks." Claire pouted, pressing her folded arms tighter against her torso.

"Claire, you *have* to trust me. When have I ever given you a reason not to believe me?"

Claire defiantly ignored him.

Harvey immediately turned to Stan. "Please tell her there's *nothing* between me and Mercedes! Tell her!"

"He doesn't have to explain anything to me. I already know what type of dog you are. Listen, dude, I don't hold it against you. My sister just has the Midas touch. I get it. She's young and fun and pretty. Has way more spunk than I do." Claire was on the verge of tears. "You're just one more thing added to the list of things she's taken from me. Because I was never as vibrant or sexy as she was. Enjoy her—"

"Claire! I don't want her! I want *you!*"

"How can I have faith in that?"

"Stan, you better tell her the truth or I swear to God, I will expose every last one of your little secrets on social media. This show will get shut down and won't get renewed for another season. And I'm *not* bluffing." Harvey whipped out his phone as if he was about to do the deed right then and there.

"Using extortion to get out the doghouse, huh? Pathetic ploy to say the least. Don't you know I have enough pull and legal resources to counter literally everything you say? I would destroy you in court. Please, let's not start down a road of humiliation—"

"Okay, ya know what? I don't have time for this." Harvey jumped up at once and stormed out of Stan's office. "Phoebe! Phoebe!" he yelled.

Phoebe was one of the nicer producers of the show. Although she concurred with a lot of the crazy procedures and unethical decisions that were carried out by her colleagues, she still had a heart for the cast members. Out of the whole production crew, she was the most approachable and handled everyone the fairest. And she actually took time to listen to the cast versus forcing her ideals down their throats.

"Phoebe!" Harvey shouted once more. She suddenly came running from a control room with a clipboard in hand.

“Yes, Harvey? I was reviewing last week’s footage.” Phoebe jotted something down on her paper. She was an interesting blend of nerd and tomboy.

“I need to borrow you for a second. I need you to tell Claire that that footage of me and Mercedes was strategically placed to make her jealous.”

Phoebe returned an apologetic face. “Harvey, it’s kinda pointless to try and convince her. She’s already made up her mind that she wants to leave the show. We just gotta figure out how we’re gonna work this around to make it make sense for the viewers when this airs. It’s far too late to start fresh—”

“Phoebe, please.” Harvey’s voice turned soft and pleading. “You’re probably my only hope right now. Claire respects you and trusts you. If she hears it from you, I think it’ll make an impression. Please do this for me,” he sniffed. “I don’t wanna lose her.”

Phoebe stood there thinking long and hard about it. She finally conceded. “Alright, I’ll try. But only because this seems to mean a lot to you.”

“Thank you, Phoebe. Thank you so much.”

Phoebe walked into Stan's office, going straight for what she was commissioned to do. "Claire, let's talk. Out in the hallway." Claire reluctantly got up to follow Phoebe outside.

"What's up?" Claire asked, folding her arms again.

"Hey listen, that whole thing with Harvey and Mercedes was…engineered for drama. I can assure you that there's nothing going on between them. You can believe me. I have no reason to lie about that. The other producer, Brent, called them up and asked them to meet at a certain location for a preliminary promo taping or some bologna like that. Just an excuse to get them together. And Stan, I believe, was the one who told Mercedes to kinda throw herself at Harvey."

"Was Harvey in on the plot too?"

"I don't think he was, Claire. I think he was the oblivious deer in that situation."

"In the footage, it looked like he was enjoying it, though."

"Listen, over the course of filming this show with you guys, I've gotten to know Harvey pretty well. I think he was just trying not to be rude when she came onto him like that. I don't think he's that type of guy, Claire. I feel like he was caught up in the moment, and honestly didn't know how to react. Behind the scenes, all he talks about is you. He's got love for no one else *but* you."

Claire could detect sincerity in Phoebe's eyes. "Positive?"

"Yes. Harvey really cares about you, more than you know. He felt like he was about to lose you for good."

"Really?"

"Yeah. Go in there and talk to him," Phoebe nudged. She went back in the control room to continue looking at footage.

Claire cautiously made her way back into Stan's office, smiling at Harvey. She felt both relieved and guilty for jumping to conclusions. Harvey glanced up at her, his eyes begging for her forgiveness.

“Harvey,” she breathed. “I believe you now.” She took a seat next to him and held his hand.

“See? I wasn’t lying to you.” His voice dropped lower so that Stan wouldn’t hear. “She explain everything to you?”

Claire simply nodded and darted her eyes over at Stan to make sure he wasn’t picking up on their clandestine communication. He sat with his fingers interlocked into each other, his brow furrowed with vexation.

“Stan, could you give us a second, please?” Harvey asked.

Stan inhaled hesitantly. “Sure, but we gotta discuss the filming schedule for these last few months, so don’t be too long.” He rose and exited his own office, closing the door behind him. It was the least he could do for putting his two stars through the ringer, especially after withholding the truth from Claire.

“Now that he’s gone, we can talk more openly,” Harvey said, peering over at the door every so often for signs of his re-entry.

"Harvey, you know I believe you now, right?"

"Yeah, I'd hope so."

"Well I can't help but wonder why it looked like you were okay with Mercedes getting so close to you. That image of you smiling while she was all up under you is really bothering me."

"Claire, I honestly had no idea that she was gonna do all that. We were told by production that we were filming a promo to advertise the show. And they did tell us to look as though we were kinda interested in each other. They wanted some clips that would incite drama or make the audience guess, ya know? Like ooooh, Harvey chose one woman to be a surrogate mother for his child, but he's pushing up on another one. You know, that whole deal. Something to keep the audience watching. It was nothing for real."

"But why didn't you just stop her and say, 'Look, you're taking this a little too far. We don't have to look *that* comfortable with each other?'"

"Well because, in the moment, it felt like the right thing to do, to let her just do her thing. I didn't agree with what she was doing, but in my mind, I justified it by saying that this would be good for the footage. Little did I know that the producers would go behind my back and show *you* the footage. I guess they were trying to turn you against me so we could have drama, too. Producers are so desperate for ratings, man. I bet you they won't even air those clips of me and Mercedes on TV. They probably filmed it just for the purpose of getting you upset."

Suddenly, the door clicked open, and in walked Stan looking as entitled as ever. "You guys finish with your little session?"

"Yeah, we're done now that you came back in," Harvey quipped.

"Well that's quite alright, Mr. Grace. Alright, let's get down to brass tax." He pulled out his massive smart phone the size of a mini tablet and immediately started punching around on it. "Okay, so…we'll be at the finish line before you know it. Claire's baby will be due in about six months…"

"I had no idea how late this baby was coming! We started filming back in what, early March? Baby should be here no later than December or a little before." Harvey wasn't ignorant to the timeline of Claire's pregnancy. Secretly, he knew something was amiss but didn't want to voice it until the opportunity presented itself. Now he felt was as good a time as any to express his concern.

Claire's stomach somersaulted within her. What Harvey said completely caught her off guard. That issue hadn't been raised in months, so for him to resurrect it was like a sudden blow to the gut. It was just one of those things she hoped would never resurface. After all, was it that big a deal whether she was pregnant at precisely the time when she was supposed to be? As long as she was going to have an actual baby, that should have been all that mattered. At least she wasn't stuffing her shirt with pillows. Prior to this, she had already kind of resolved in her head to not even tell him the truth at the reunion or after taping wrapped. She concluded that in the grand scheme of things, that detail of her pregnancy was inconsequential.

But the more she gazed upon how naive Harvey was as to why her baby was due later than expected, the more she felt bad. And the more she reasoned that he deserved to know the truth, especially after he proved his honesty to her.

"Harvey, I need to tell you something," she started, looking down apprehensively.

Stan cut her a look which she could feel without even directly looking at him. She knew she was about to renege on their deal, but she had to do it. She would not be able to live with herself and continue in a relationship with Harvey if she kept this a secret forever.

"Harvey…I wasn't exactly pregnant when you chose me to be the surrogate mother."

A very heavy cloud of silence descended on the room. Harvey's face was virtually expressionless, as he was in a limbo of emotions. It took all of five minutes for her revelation to register with him. "Wait, what? Did you just say—"

"Yes, Harvey. I was not pregnant. My main reason for being on this show was to make some extra money. I was in somewhat of an unhappy place in my life, and—"

"But you *are* pregnant now, right? I mean, that'd be one heck of a hoax if you weren't. Your acting would be too convincing."

"Yeah. I, uh—Stan made me go get an AI."

"An artificial insemination?"

"Yup. And so I've been pregnant since like mid-April."

Stan shook his head in displeasure of what she had done. Harvey stared at Claire intently, trying to sort in his mind how he should evaluate this situation. At the forefront of his concerns was the fact that she lied to him, manipulated producers to get on the show, and deprived thousands of pregnant hopefuls of a spot. The other thing was that now he would have to wait *later* to get his prize, his baby. But then the bigger part of him kept thinking that it really didn't matter *when* she got pregnant. As long as there was *something* in the oven waiting to come out. He eventually arrived at the conclusion that getting upset over a delayed pregnancy was petty. Even though Claire was untruthful with him in the beginning, he wouldn't hold it against her because what mattered was right now.

"You know, you didn't have to tell me this. I mean, we're so deep in that it's kinda pointless. Not to mitigate your honesty at all, but I'm just saying that after all we've been through, it's relatively small."

Claire was really surprised that this was his reaction. She anticipated that he would storm out and want nothing to do with her ever again. But she got just the opposite. She smiled with relief that he wasn't mad at her.

"My mom used to always recite that verse in the Bible to me and my sisters, the one that says that the person who is faithful in what is least is also faithful in much. I think it was somewhere in Luke chapter sixteen. That phrase always stuck with me, because I found it to be true in almost every situation in my life."

"Why does that have significance right now?" Harvey asked.

"Because like you just said, what I revealed to you was relatively small. And I agree. Initially, I didn't feel that way, though. After I built up the nerve to tell Stan the truth, I felt like you especially deserved to know it, if not more than him. But he told me not to tell you right away. He wanted me to wait until the show finished taping." Stan slouched in his seat a little from guilt. "But then the more I thought about it, the more I realized that it really wasn't that big a deal. You were still going to get your baby at the end of this, and we would never see each other again anyway. My point is, though, that me telling you this 'small' thing is my way of showing you that I can be honest and faithful in big things. I really value your trust, and I do hope that we can continue our friendship when this is long over."

"That's actually something I've wanted to talk to you about," Harvey began. "Claire, I feel like both of us have been sweeping our feelings for each other under the rug. We never really addressed me saying 'I love you.' I truly do care about you. But I may have been a little too hasty when I said those three magic words. Looking back, I don't think those feelings were love per se but infatuation. I got so accustomed to spending time with you, I became attracted to your personality and wanted your company. But I can't say that that was truly love."

Harvey was divulging his true emotions tenderly, but to Claire, it still felt like small daggers piercing her heart. It was disappointing to hear that he didn't think he was actually in love with her. She had been debating with herself for a while prior to him "confessing his love" if he felt the same way about her as she did him. He saying he loved her wasn't enough benediction. This whole time, she tried to mask her real feelings for him, because she wasn't sure if the feelings were mutual. And here was confirmation that they weren't. Now there was no point in telling him that she actually did love him. To the extent that she wouldn't mind spending the rest of her life with him.

"So…if you're not in love with me, then what can we call this thing we have?" Claire's eyes began to turn glassy. "Because that day when I fought Mercedes, I told her that we had something." She choked a little, almost regretting that she jumped the gun and said anything. She felt stupid for placing a title on their relationship when all this time, Harvey wasn't genuinely in love with her.

"You didn't let me finish. That was my prelude to what I really wanna say. Having spent more time with you and *really* getting to know you, I came to develop *real* love for you. I can honestly tell you that I'm truly, madly, deeply in love with you."

"Explain to me what the difference between love and infatuation is though. I wanna know what that entails," Claire demanded.

"Infatuation is an obsession with someone, you can't get them off your mind. You constantly wonder what they're doing every minute of every day. Everything you do, you think about how they would feel about it if they were there. But it's like, when the novelty wears off and the interest is gone, there's nothing. There's no spark." He paused to caress Claire's face. "But love—love is merely infatuation times infinity. It's literally forever. The novelty never wears off because love causes you to constantly see things about your soul mate. The butterflies never go away. The spark never fizzles out. It stands the test of time. You know me, Claire, I'm not the most avid Bible reader, but, uh, I actually decided to give the Bible a shot one day. And I was reading that verse that you told me about, about how love is patient. Well I read further and something else in that chapter caught my eye. It said that love endures all things and that it never fails."

Claire was swept off her feet. "That's impressive," she said softly.

Harvey turned to Stan. "Stan, I love Claire. I'm really glad you guys casted her to be on this show." He and Claire chuckled. "When she has the baby, I'm going to ask her to be the mother of my—*our*—child."

Claire's jaw dropped open. Her eyes became like quivering reflective pools. "Wait, you want to be a family?"

"Yes, Claire. I can't picture my life without you. I wanna spend my future with you and our beautiful baby…baby…"

"Oh my goodness! I'm so happy!" Claire was ecstatic. Just when she thought that Harvey didn't love her, he dropped this bomb. She had no idea that his feelings really did run as deep as hers.

"You're a smart cookie, Harvey. This is gonna get a crap ton of ratings. Good thinking," Stan complimented.

"Hold on, you aren't just doing this for the views, right?" Claire wanted to know.

"No, of course not! I promise you this is for real. In fact, I have a ring to consecrate that promise, too." He reached into his back pocket and pulled out a black velvet box, opening it up to reveal a modest, but sparkly, ring.

Claire gasped and cupped her mouth with her hands. "It's beautiful!"

"I'm glad you love it. This is a symbol of my undying love for you," Harvey replied melodramatically.

"Okay, okay folks. Let's not get soap opera-y around here! Please, save the sap for when we actually film this episode," Stan teased. "Oh, and no rings exchanged right now! Save that for the last episode, too!"

Chapter 10

Claire felt like she was literally roasting in an inferno. Between the hot lights above her in the hospital room, her own skyrocketed temperature from the strenuous labor, and the overheating camera equipment, it was the most conflagrant she'd ever felt in her life. But it would all be over once her baby girl mustered the strength to push her way into the world. Tabitha would be her name. Tabitha Geraldine Grace. Harvey requested that his daughter have his mother's first name. It was his way of honoring her memory.

All that could be heard were frantic exchanges between the doctors and Claire struggling to force Tabitha out of her. The production crew was mute and so was Harvey as they stood on the sidelines watching the childbirth unfold. The camera guy got closer to the action once the doctors announced that the baby's head was visible. Claire squeezed her mom's hand looking down at the lens inching towards the inside of her legs. The last thing she needed at this arduous time was a camera violating her personal space.

“Aaauuggh! You guys better edit out those shots of my crotch, Stan, I swear!” Claire grunted. She clenched her mom’s hand even harder with agitation.

“Claire, I already told you this very moment was going to be raw and unadulterated with very little editing. You agreed to this when you signed your name on that dotted line. Sorry,” Stan apologized matter-of-factly.

Claire strained to raise her head to listen to him, her neck wrinkled like an accordion and drenched in sweat. She could move nothing below her shoulders. “Yeah, but I didn’t think you guys were gonna get *this* up close and personal. Gosh!” She slammed her head back down onto the pillow, which was totally soaked in her perspiration.

“Oh, we planned on doing things a lot differently than these other televised births,” Stan explained. “We gotta stand out! We can’t have viewers thinking this is just another cheap delivery story!”

“I know, but do you *have* to be different at the expense of my dignity? Can’t you at least blur out some stuff?” Claire asked, hoping she could reach a compromise with the man who had been giving her hell over the course of this entire taping.

"Of course it's gonna get blurred out! There's certain imagery that will never be okay for TV, and this is one of 'em. Besides, the network thinks this kinda stuff is 'too graphic' for general audiences, because they do want us to appeal to families overall," Stan said mockingly. "But my thing is, just throw up a disclaimer at the beginning of *this* particular episode, and we should be fine!"

"Stan, just—thank you for blurring out my crotch. I appreciate it." Claire wasn't up for going back and forth with him. So she decided to put her weapons down and back away. Her main concern was getting Tabitha out. "Okay, baby girl! I gave you your eviction notice! It's time for you to pack up and move out. Like today!"

The whole room roared with laughter. "Girl, you crazy!" Geraldine said, still clutching her daughter's hand. A warm smile formed on her face as it just hit her that she was about to be a grandmother.

"It's nice to see that even under this extreme pressure, your daughter still has a sense of humor," the doctor said, beaming at the two lovely ladies. He tended back to Tabitha who was just about half way out. “Keep pushing, Claire. She’s almost outta there.” Claire drew in a heavy breath and pushed it out of her mouth putting her Lamaze classes to good use. “That’s it. Do it a few more times, Claire.” She obliged, grimacing in pain as the camera guy eased in without her knowledge.

“Just gotta get her other foot out,” the doctor said. A few seconds later, the room filled with the ear-shattering cries of a newborn infant. She was finally here. A beautiful baby girl. Claire lifted her head scrunching her neck to see her tiny bundle of joy. The doctor clipped the umbilical cord and immediately went to wrap her up.

“I wanna see her,” Claire cried, repositioning herself to sit more upright.

“Sure.” The doctor brought Tabitha over to her and gently placed her in Claire’s arms. The baby creaked and whined, her little hands trembling in the air. She was covered in grey gook which made her look like an alien. Claire wiped away some of the slime from Tabitha’s face and tenderly kissed her on the forehead.

"She's gorgeous," Claire said, tears welling up in her eyes. The smile of a mother spread across her face. "Harvey, come take a look."

Harvey shyly stepped forward in front of the camera, as it pulled back to make room for his entrance. He stared at Tabitha for the longest time, in utter disbelief that this small life would be his to take care of for the next eighteen years or beyond. The shock of being a father was so overwhelming that it made him a bit standoffish towards his daughter. He stood kind of aloof.

"Harvey, come closer. Look at how beautiful your daughter is. She's gonna have amazing hair." Claire laughed, playfully poking at Tabitha's nose. She planted another kiss, but this time on her chubby cheek.

Harvey edged forward a little more and leaned in to get a better look at the baby. His walls slowly started to come down as he watched this cute innocent human squeal and stir within Claire's arms. "She is a beauty."

"And she's yours," Claire replied, gleaming up at Harvey. Her glow faded when she looked back down at Tabitha, sad in knowing that they would have to part soon.

Even though Claire knew that she wouldn't be away from her daughter forever, the thought of Tabitha being separated from her after nine months in her womb was saddening. She wondered how any mother was strong enough to deal with that, to have a living person that was inside of you for so long be taken out of you. It felt like a piece of your existence was stripped away.

The camera guy got closer to Harvey's face. Claire tried not to have any emotion, as she already knew what was about to happen. The room got real silent as if on cue for what Harvey was going to say. The sound guy inched forward lowering the boom slightly to pick up everything that came out of Harvey's mouth. "He's *ours*," Harvey declared. Claire flashed an ambiguous grin, one that was passable enough to show the audience that she was pleasantly surprised and to satisfy her genuine feelings in that moment.

"Claire, I don't want this to just be *my* baby. I want the three of us to be a family," Harvey said softly, caressing Tabitha's hair.

Claire could tell that there was something more that Harvey wanted to say because of his body language and how the cameras were closing in on them little by little. *What else does he need to tell me,* she thought. He already revealed that he wants her to stay in the baby's life. This was the climactic scene that Stan wanted, so it should be done. The crew can pack up and leave now. But when she realized that something else was around the corner, it made her nervous to the point where she began lightly bouncing Tabitha in her arms. Her eyes were fixed to Harvey. Her heart was racing. She didn't know what bomb he was going to drop. This show was full of surprises and turns. The hormones still in effect, a bunch of possibilities ran through her mind at once.

What if her Harvey-Mercedes love connection theory was true and her annoying little sister popped out at any minute? Or what if Harvey revealed that he was gay and wanted Claire as part of a weird, extended family? Then she thought of the likelihood that Harvey would pull one of those unfinished-sentences-that-end-up-being-letdowns. Maybe he was going to say that he wanted the three of them to be a family, but it wouldn't work out. Or that he regrets his decision to have her be the surrogate mother and wants to start over, and that would be the setup for a second season. But if it was the last option, then that's really low, she thought to herself. You don't string someone along for *that long*, just to drop them like a bad habit. All of these crazy speculations filled her head in anticipation for what he was about to say.

"Claire. At the beginning of our journey together on this show, you know I was strongly opposed to the idea of finding true love. I thought it was implausible to find a better half, someone that you can trust. But then you showed me that love can be found in the most unlikely places…even on a TV show." He paused and approached closer to Claire. A doctor's assistant came to take the baby away from her. She looked up at Harvey with wide, expectant eyes as he reached into his back pocket and pulled out a folded sheet of paper. He opened it up and waited a beat before he started reading from it.

"Love is patient and kind," he said, staring at Claire with familiar eyes. "You taught me that I have to wait for true love to come to me. I can't just give up after so many failed attempts. And I think I can stop looking now." He gave her a heartening smile. "You were so kind to me in the beginning, even though I was so resistant to the idea of love." He came even closer to her, taking her hand.

"Love is not jealous. Initially, I didn't know if you fit this bill, because of the whole Mercedes thing—" Claire giggled. "—but then I realized that you didn't let jealousy consume you. At one point, you even told me to enjoy her and seemed ready to move on. Love does not brag. You never bragged about anything. You're one of the most humble people I know. Love does not get puffed up. Even when you were mad at me, your ego never got the best of you. Love does not behave indecently. Ignoring the brawl you had with your sister, you carry yourself with such maturity and sophistication. You're a class act in my book. Love does not look for its own interests. You are not concerned with self. You took the time to listen to me and be there for me when I confided in you. Love does not become provoked. Again, the Mercedes thing had me doubting if this applied to you—" Claire laughed again, a tear falling down her cheek. "—but one thing I can say is that you never flew off the handle with *me*. Love does not keep account of the injury. Although I may have done things to offend you, you eventually overlooked them. And I appreciate you for not holding them against me. Love does not rejoice over unrighteousness, it bears all things, believes all things, hopes all things, and endures all things. Love never fails." His voice cracked with emotion at the very end. He gazed into Claire's eyes which were brimming with tears. "Taken from First Corinthians chapter thirteen and verses four through eight," he finished, folding the paper back up.

The entire hospital room was overtaken with quiet. It seemed like even the miscellaneous sounds of equipment, medical and production, were muted for this very moment.

"Claire. You fit every last one of these things that describe love. And…I know beyond a shadow of a doubt that you are the one I'm supposed to have. All these signs point to you." He sat on the edge of her bed and grabbed both her arms. "Claire, will you be my one and only forever and ever?"

The moment he asked her this, her breath was stolen. She peered into his piercing blue eyes which shivered with eagerness. "Yes. Yes, I would love to be your one and only." The waterworks could not contain themselves. Before long, tears were streaming down her cheeks, as if buckets of sweat from every pore on her face weren't enough.

*****

It had been four months since the show wrapped filming. Tonight was the night that Claire and Harvey would get to see almost a year of their lives played out before millions of people on television. For Claire, the feeling was surreal. She had never done anything like this in her life. For Harvey, being on a reality TV show was nothing new. But the experience of this show was unlike anything he had done before. Both of them were anxious to see how the producers were going to chop and screw the footage, to fit their predetermined storyline. They wondered what rude and hateful comments they would get on their social media pages, and which memes would be made about their precious little daughter, Tabitha at the end of the season. Harvey already warned her of how ruthless people can be to reality stars, in person *and* virtually.

'Let's Make a Baby' was going to premiere in about four hours, and the anticipation for it was at an all time high in the Grace-Rexall household. They had invited a few close friends and family over for a little viewing party. Claire wanted to go all out for the event. She hired a caterer to provide deli trays, wings, nachos, shrimp baskets, the whole shebang. Tabitha would be put to sleep when the party started so the adults could play.

"What flavor wings are we gonna have?" Harvey asked, positioning the 80-inch Nakimoto TV just right in their living room. It was one of those massive, cinematic-type curved televisions with like 8K resolution. The thing cost a fortune. But it complimented their living area quite nicely, and it's not like Harvey didn't inherit billions of dollars from his parents. With all that money, Harvey decided to move him and his family into a new place. A 4,090 square foot penthouse loft in the Gibraltar District of Casa Nueva, California. That affluent community, just sixty miles north of San Diego, was home to some of the best pieces of real estate in the entire country. And it was definitely one of the lesser known places to live.

"Um, I decided on garlic parmesan, teriyaki, Thai curry, sweet habanero, and honey barbecue," Claire replied, un-bagging some groceries.

"What about zesty ranch? You can't forget that. That's my favorite, babe," he said.

"No, honey, you know that flavor is really high in sodium and we need to watch your salt intake. Can't have your blood pressure through the roof," she reminded.

Harvey chuckled. “Why do you make us sound like an old couple that’s been married for forty plus years? Honey, yer know this stuff isn’t good fer ya. It’ll throw yer diabetes into a kizzy,” he said, mocking the voice of an old married woman. “We’re too young to care about stuff like blood pressure and heart disease.”

“You are so crazy!” Claire shook her head at the nut she was about to be married to in less than two months. “I can’t believe you! You know these health problems can affect anybody, right?”

“Well we’ll try to avoid them as much as we humanly can,” he replied with a cheesy wink.

“Right, and it starts with eliminating zesty anything from our diet,” she quipped.

“But come on, baaaabe. It tastes so good!” he cried, whining like a begging toddler. He came into the kitchen and wrapped his arms around Claire’s body from the back. Then he slowly started smooching on the base of her neck, making a trail all the way to her shoulder and back again.

"Is this your way of getting me to cave?" Claire asked, trying her hardest to not show that she was enjoying this. She had to control herself from gasping with ecstasy. The tingles that traveled down her spine were too much.

"Is it working?" Harvey asked, bringing his body closer to hers.

His cologne entered her lungs, so sweet and enticing like a love potion, that made her want to say yes and to keep going. "If I answer that—"

Before she could even finish her sentence, Harvey turned her around and lifted her up onto the kitchen counter. He placed himself in between her legs and started kissing her again on the face. He began sweet talking her, smooching after every word. "You (smooch) taste (smooch) so (smooch) scrumptious (smooch), my little chocolate drop."

Claire's head dropped back in sheer elation. He was taking her to a place she only wanted to go after dark. "Harvey," she whispered. Suddenly, the doorbell rang.

Harvey stopped and sighed with irritation. "Really? Who could that possibly be? You're lucky, girl. You were saved by the bell." He headed for the door. Claire sighed with relief because she knew she wouldn't have been able to restrain herself too much longer if he had kept going.

Harvey glanced through the peephole and jerked his head back in surprise. "What's Tanya doing here so early?" He unlocked the door and opened it, greeted by a busty blonde woman with exaggerated makeup. "Hi, Tanya," Harvey said through gritted teeth. He resented her for ruining a moment.

"Hey, cousin!" she replied excitedly, flashing the biggest smile. "Sorry for being so early, but I tried to find stuff to keep me occupied up until seven, but I couldn't do it. So I decided what the hey. I'll just drop by my favorite little cousin's house a little early. I'm sure he won't mind. You don't mind, right?"

"Of course not! Make yourself at home," he lied, still clenching his teeth. "Claire and I totally had nothing going on." His sarcasm was starting to ooze out.

Claire cut him a look to behave. "Get comfortable, Tanya. You're here kinda early for food and refreshments, but I got some grapes you could munch on before the real stuff gets here."

"Oh. You don't have any juice or soda or anything I can drink?"

Claire slapped her wrist. "Where are my manners? The first thing I should've asked you is if you wanted something to drink. Where is my head at?" Of course, Claire was being facetious with her. She knew just how imposing Harvey's cousin could be and found that the best way to deal with her was to just acquiesce to her every demand. Then she won't ask as much.

Tanya certainly obliged both Claire and Harvey by making herself comfortable. She kicked off her wedges and grabbed the remote from off the glass coffee table in front of the couch. "I wanna see you guys now!" she exclaimed, flicking on the TV.

"Um, Tanya, you *do* realize the show doesn't come on until eight tonight, right?" Claire asked, pouring a glass of cranberry apple juice.

"No, silly. They're showing a two-minute sneak peak of the show. Were you not aware of that?"

"What? Stan didn't tell us about a sneak peek!" Harvey said, flying onto the couch to see it. Claire joined them, practically shoving the glass of juice into Tanya's hand.

'The Rich Chicks of Belgium' was just ending when a teaser for 'Let's Make a Baby' popped up on the screen. "*Get ready for an exclusive preview of the brand new series, 'Let's Make a Baby' which starts in 5…4…3…2…1.*"

The screen went black and opened back up with a shot of a pregnant Claire ambling her way to a table. The setup looked familiar to Claire. "Wait, is this the infamous rooftop incident?" Claire asked, sitting up to better see. The scene cut to her taking a seat and then another jump cut to Harvey taking a seat. Then another jump cut to Mercedes walking towards the table and a jump cut to her sitting down with them. The arrangement of the shots was purposely jarring, to create tension and make the audience feel like something bad was about to happen.

"I really wish she wasn't here right now. Like just seeing her face is making my blood boil," Claire's voice said over a shot of her scowling at Mercedes.

"I'm looking at this girl just walk up to me, and I have no idea who she is and why she's here," Harvey's voice said. A shot of Mercedes introducing herself to Harvey was shown. Both snippets of Claire and Harvey's voices were from their interviews with producers.

What followed was a confusing sequence of shots from the argument leading up to that fateful squabble between Claire and Mercedes. It was incoherently strung together to throw the viewers off and make them want to watch to see what's going on. The music gradually intensified as the camera switched back and forth from Claire to Mercedes. It culminated with very abrupt clips of Claire pulling her sister's hair and a barrage of bleeps. The screen glitched to reveal the hashtag '#WhoIsShe,' in reference to Mercedes. Then it went back to Claire throwing silverware at Mercedes, and cut to the title of the show.

"Woooow," Tanya said astonished.

"Yeah, Tanya. You see what I'm marrying, right?" Harvey cracked.

"Shut up, Harvey!" Claire said, smacking him on the back with a pillow.

The end.

A New Start

When a tragedy leads to them coming together...

When Andrea took a dream PR job at Wade Enterprises, she never expected to get romantic interest from Michael Wade himself!

With a reputation as a playboy billionaire, while he has the looks and money every girl dreams of, Andrea needs more.

Little did she know, more is what she was going to get.

After the tragic death of his father, Michael has to step up and take care of the family business.

This new found responsibility didn't only stop at work, but also carried through to his personal life and made him just the man Andrea was looking for.

But when Andrea finds herself pregnant with Michael's child, will things all become too much for the previously care free billionaire?

Find out in this emotional and clean (no adult scenes) romance story by Mary Peart of BWWM Club.

Contents

Chapter 1

It had been two months since they had gotten the horrible and shocking news that the private plane carrying Michael Wade the first had crashed into the Atlantic Ocean; there had been no survivors.

The offices still had a hushed funeral atmosphere about it as the entire staff including board members, waited to hear what was going to happen. Today was the day. The funeral had been a private affair with family members, a few close friends and business associates. The towering high rise building that housed Wade Enterprises had held a memorial service for the staff.

Andrea Williams shifted some documents around on her desk absently. She had seen them go into the massive board room; his wife, the beautiful and elegant Gloria Wade and his son Michael Wade II, whom she had seen flitting through the offices in the past with a different woman trailing on his arm. Tall, raven haired, intense green eyes and tanned skin that spoke of many lazy days in the sun; he had most of the female staff at Wade Enterprises sighing in longing; except Andrea who had no time for the idle rich. She had only caught a glimpse of him as he led his mother towards the room but he looked like his father's death had dealt him a terrible blow. He no longer looked carefree and reckless but had a serious and sad expression on his too handsome face.

She had liked the father as had everyone. He treated them with the utmost courtesy and had being a more than fair employer. She had worked closely with him and had spent many a late evening with him bouncing off ideas about the image of the company.

Andrea gave a sigh as she stood and reached for the current folder she had been working on that had been put on hold for the time being. The company had acquired a pharmaceutical company that had been ailing for years and needed a massive face lift. She had drawn up a few ideas and had been going it over with him the week before he died. He had decided to get rid of the management of the company and a few staff members and revitalize the entire pharmaceutical company. The name would remain the same but the slogan: 'We provide for all your health needs' would be shelved and Andrea had come up with: 'Your healthcare is in our hands' and he had approved it; now she would have to wait and see what the person in charge was going to do about it; about everything.

She had her own office; a large ultra-modern room complete with a mini fridge, a microwave and a big oval shaped desk that had her desktop computer, printer and facsimile machine. She was very good at her job and was compensated handsomely for her expertise.

“I wish I could look as calm and sane as you do right now.” Thirty six year old cool and attractive Millie came into her office. She had been Mr. Wade’s personal secretary for more than ten years and had guarded his office like a mother bear protecting her young one.

“I doubt that you have anything to worry about,” Andrea said dryly with a fond smile as she came into the office and sat on one of the chairs in front of the desk; crossing elegant legs. “You’re practically an institution here,” she added teasingly. She had come on board two years ago and Millie had taken her under her wing much to the envy of the administrative staff; which she treated with veiled contempt.

“I never take anything for granted honey,” she said with a twinkle in her bright blue eyes. Her blonde hair was cut in a fashionable bob and she dressed as if she had just stepped from a fashion magazine. Andrea started taking fashion advice from her a few months after she had been hired and had been transformed into a tall, slim and curvaceous woman with minimum make-up on her caramel face. Her dark brown eyes were highlighted by the flesh tone highlighter she used and her full lips were shown to full advantage with a soft orange red lip gloss. They were as different as night and day but had become very good friends.

“Who do you think is going to be at the helm?” Andrea asked curiously. She never encouraged office gossip and Millie was the only one she felt confident enough to indulge in it.

“Maybe young Michael,” Millie said with an elegant shrug.

Andrea raised tapered brows. “Does he know anything about running the company?”

“With an MBA from Harvard he should,” Millie said ruefully. “Underneath that slutty exterior he is quite smart.”

Andrea laughed in amusement. “Lord help us,” she said with a fatalistic shrug.

There was a commotion outside the office just then and the two women looked out to see the board members and the Wade's leaving.

"I guess we will know more shortly," Millie said, standing in one graceful movement. "I'll let you know." She headed for the door.

Andrea watched them leave and saw Michael stop to say something to Grace from accounts. The woman laughed breathlessly and touched him on the arm; her hand lingering; the woman was a walking advertisement for marriage, Andrea thought distastefully as Grace stood there watching Michael leave. She had on too much make-up and her clothes were too tight and she appeared to be very false. Idiot! Andrea thought impatiently, returning her attention to the file she had on her desk.

*****

"That woman is a disgrace to women everywhere," Gloria Wade said to her son as soon as they were in the elevator. She looked a little tired but apart from that she was elegance personified with her rich blonde hair and intense blue eyes and her delicate creamy complexion was still quite youthful.

“Be nice mother,” Michael reproved her gently as they stepped off the elevator and went towards the large glass doors which were being pushed open by the doorman. They gave him a friendly nod and stepped out into the bright sunlight where the white BMW was waiting for them. The chauffeur sprang into action and opened the passenger door so that they could enter.

“I am being nice,” Gloria retorted settling back against the soft leather upholstery and stretching her legs out. “I did not say she was a tart did I?”

Michael reached out and took one delicate hand in his own and squeezed in reassured. He knew she was facing a lot because she and her husband had been so close and to lose him so suddenly it could not be easy.

“It’s not going to be easy taking over the realms Michael,” she turned to her son and looked at him in concern. His father had been so concerned about his lifestyle and had wondered if he would ever settle down and take responsibilities for his life. They had spoiled him too much and looking the way he did with women falling at his feet, did not make it any better. Hopefully now this sad situation would make him settle down.

“I know Mom,” he told her a little grimly. He had spent the entire time in the board room and seen rather than heard, the contempt and scant regards the board had of him; not that he could blame them entirely; he had never contributed anything towards the building up of the company and it was through inheritance rather than hard work that had made him head of a company that his father and the board had worked so hard to make it what it was today. He knew he would have to spend some time proving himself to a group of men who were old enough to be his father. “I won’t let him down,” he added quietly.

Gloria covered his hand with hers and settling back, closed her eyes; her thoughts drifting to the last time she had spoken to her husband.

“I wished you wouldn’t go darling. You should be scaling back now instead you’re flying all over the place.” She had complained as she wrapped her hands around his neck and stared up at him. They had been together since she was eighteen and he was twenty and had worked with him and supported him in building the company from the ground up. There had been a shaky moment when he had gotten involved with his secretary but she had straightened that out and it had never happened again. Their union had produced only Michael II and she had hoped there would be more; even a daughter but that had not happened and she had poured all her love on her only child.

“You know I have to make this deal by myself,” he had told her, planting a tender kiss on her lips. The kiss had led to him being an hour late for his flight. She was not sure how she was going to survive without him; the thought flashed through her and she quelled the tears threatening to spill; she had to be there for their son and help him in whatever way she could.

*****

Andrea was nervous and she hated being nervous; especially due to the fact that she had already proven herself as being a very good PRO and now it felt like she had to do it all over again. The word was out: Michael, the son, was now the new CEO of Wade Enterprises and was now occupying his father's office. Michelle had told her in confidence that he seemed to know what he was about so maybe he was not just another pretty face.

She smoothed down the chic pin striped pant suit she had worn with a white silk shirt underneath. Her short cropped brown hair was liberally streaked with blonde and her make-up flawless as usual. She had certainly not dressed to impress him but it would surely do no harm in looking her best.

Michelle had called and told her that he was ready to see her now. Andrea gathered her files and headed to the suite of offices that had been Michael Wade the first. She had been there many times for meetings but the opulence never failed to impress her. His offices took up one whole section and consisted of an outer office that served as a waiting area with refreshments on a long trestle table, a coffee pot that was constantly ready, tea and of course several choices of juices. There were also a dozen comfortable chairs for visitors to sit and wait and a large flat screen television secured to the wall. Michelle's office was large and luxurious with white carpeting that you could sink your feet in and felt as if you were walking on a cloud. She was on the telephone and indicated with a smile and a wave of her hand for Andrea to go on in.

He had not changed anything; not that anything needed changing and Andrea felt the pull of sorrow as she saw him seated around the massive oak desk where his father used to be.

“Ms. Williams please have a seat,” he told her cordially. He was dressed in a light blue shirt and the sleeves were rolled up revealing dark hairs on his forearm. “I understand you have been working on the damage control for the pharmaceutical company we acquired; how soon can we go ahead and make a statement to the press?”

Andrea felt herself bristling. His father would have been jovial and asked her how her day was going and when she was going to give him the secret to her success but he was not his father and that was fine by her.

“We cannot go to the press until the terms of the contract has been ironed out and there’s still the question of who in the company has been distributing drugs illegally,” she told him coolly.

“Do you think I can run this company Ms. Williams?” he asked her suddenly. He leaned forward and placed his forearms on the desk. The two buttons on his shirt were undone and she caught a glimpse of the dark hair there.

“Excuse me?” she asked him.

“A wager has been set as to how soon I will run this company to the ground. What do you think?” he asked her with a quirk of his lips.

“I think it’s up to you to prove them wrong or right,” Andrea told him. She had no idea there was a wager going on but she had never participated in office gossips and found it distasteful.

“You have been highly recommended by my father, he was always talking about the great work you do for the company. ‘A good PRO makes a company shine’ he always said and you apparently do a very good job. What do you think of my image?”

“You have the wrong image for a multi-billion company and you’re going to have to change that before anyone can take you seriously.” Andrea told him bluntly. He had asked and she responded.

“You don’t pull your punches do you?” he said with a grim smile.

“I am honest and I tell people what is true, not want they want to hear.”

He looked at her for a moment; his green eyes boring into hers. Andrea looked back without flinching. He looked away first, his eyes going to the file she had given him. “I need to go over this and see where we go from here. Please tell Millie that I won’t be seeing anyone else for the rest of the day.” He told her with a dismissive smile.

Andrea stood up gracefully and headed for the door. “Ms. Williams,” his voice stopped her as soon as she reached the doorway. “I might need your help dealing with my image problem,” his voice was laced with amusement and with a nod of her head Andrea left the office.

His self-confidence needed redefining, she thought to herself. She gave Millie the message and because the woman was busy punching keys on her computer she left without further conversation.

She went back to her office and closed the door to deal with the myriad of things on her desk. Wade Enterprises had several companies they had bought and either revamped or made different and she was in charge of seeing that the image of those companies remained spotless. They had hotels, restaurants, a car dealership, and real estate agencies.

Andrea pulled out the file on the latest hotel acquisition and started writing her recommendation on how to bring it back to life. It was in a good part of town with restaurants and malls around and a lot of businesses had started up in the last few years. The renovation had started and she wanted to compile an eye catching magazine that depicted the rooms and the advantages of staying there when one was in town for business or even a restaurant, if one was simply shopping and felt the need for fine dining. She had been working with the advertising agency to come up with something compelling enough to start business rolling in.

She loved her job and spent most of her time at the office; her apartment barely looked lived in and even when she was at home, she was working on ideas for one company or the other. She had no time for a relationship and the last one had fizzled out before it had gone anywhere. She had been described as frigid and unattainable and it made no difference to her.

Her mother and father had died in a car accident when she was at college and she had vowed to make them proud of her even though they were not around.

She stretched her legs out and replace the file she had been working on in the allotted space and realized to her surprise that it was almost six 'o clock.

Millie had suggested that they took in the new restaurant that had opened up at the mall and she had said yes but she wanted to work some more on the image for the pharmaceutical company.

There was a knock on the door and she called out for the person to enter. To her surprise she saw that it was Michael. His hair was slightly disheveled as if he had been spending time running his fingers through it. “I thought I would take a walk and beard the lioness in her den,” he told her with an attractive smile. “You keep late hours.”

“So do you.” She told him, not bothering to get up as he wandered inside, looking at her. “I am learning the ropes, what's your excuse?” he leaned against her desk.

“I happen to be working,” she told him with a slight shrug.

He folded his hands across his chest, his leg swinging. “I want us to work closely together to sort out that hitch with the pharmaceutical company. I was looking at your file and I saw where you put a question sign beside David Baker's name; why is that?"

"Your father met with him a few weeks ago before the accident and he told me that he was too eager to please. He was one of the middle managers but was way too free with his information about the others in the company." Andrea told him.

He nodded. "Our P.I. managed to dig up some interesting things about Mr. Baker. He is in debt to the tune of half a million dollars; it appears he has been gambling high stakes and not very good at it." Michael said dryly. "I am meeting with him tomorrow and I want you to be present as well."

"Why?" Andrea asked him puzzled. She did not have time to be meeting with anyone, that was not her area and she had too many things to do.

"Other than the fact that I am your boss and I said so?" he looked at her in amusement. "I would like your take on it."

"You're the boss," Andrea said with a shrug.

"Why are you still here?" he asked her curiously. He had taken up a crystal paperweight from her desk and was examining it curiously. She had gotten it as a gift from his father last year when he went on a trip to France.

“What do you mean?”

“Why is a beautiful woman like you working so late?” he clarified, placing the object carefully on the desk. “No other half to go home to?”

“No, not that it’s any of your business,” Andrea told him coolly. “If I was a man you would not be asking me that question; as a matter of fact you would be commending me on my dedication to the job.”

He stared at her for a moment; his dark green eyes boring into hers and for a brief moment she thought maybe she had gone too far.

“You’re right,” he said briefly, straightening up from her desk. “Keep up the good work Ms. Williams.” Without another word he headed towards the door; closing it softly behind him.

Andrea closed her eyes in exasperation. She and her bigmouth. Her mother had often told her when she was a little girl that it was going to get her into trouble. But Michael Wade brought out the worst in her. He was everything she disliked in a man; he had not worked a day in his life and had everything handed to him on a silver platter; his parents had seen to that. Now, he had inherited a company that was going so well and who knew how he was going to deal with it. They were all up in odds about the future of the company and even though Andrea believed in giving a person the benefit of the doubt; Michael had never set foot inside the company to do an honest day's work and now he was here calling the shots. It hardly seemed fair. And besides he was way too handsome for his own good; everything came easy for him.

She pulled the pharmaceutical file and pored over the information she had acquired. The company had been doing very well until two years ago when the stocks had started to decline with many rumors about drugs going out without FDA approval and illegal drugs being a part of the set up. It was going to take a massive face lift to get it up and running again.

Chapter 2

The meeting was rescheduled and Andrea could not help but wonder if it had anything to do with what she had said to him the evening before. But Millie told her that he had to go to a meeting with one of the board members to the owner of the company they were trying to acquire.

“How is he fitting in?” Andrea asked the woman curiously. They were on their lunch break and had decided to go out and eat in a restaurant on the road near to the towering office building. It was Wednesday and there was a small crowd milling around. The weather was mild and a little muggy for the ending of summer and Andrea had chosen to wear a slim fitting red and white dress with a white fitted jacket.

They had gotten their order of tomato soup and grilled chicken sandwich and were enjoying the little break from the office.

“He seems to be fitting in quite nicely,” Millie told her with a small smile. “I had my doubts about him and had painted him as a spoiled little rich boy but I am revising my opinion. He treats me with the utmost respect and courtesy and has shown that he is not a push over.”

"Good," Andrea said biting into her sandwich. "In order to earn the respect of his board members and the business world he has to be able to show that he knows what he is doing."

Millie nodded. She was dressed in a pink and white skirt suit and her blonde hair was in an elegant chignon at the nape of her neck. "You don't like him much do you?" Millie looked at her friend in amusement.

"I just don't like what he represents." Andrea told her.

They finished eating lunch and went back to the office.

*****

The meeting was held the following day at ten o'clock sharp in his office. He gave her a barely perceptible nod when she entered his office. David Baker was already present. The man looked shifty and uncomfortable. He was middle-aged with thinning black hair and his face was florid that spoke of years of alcohol abuse.

Michael was dressed in a light pink shirt and as usual had rolled up the sleeves and unbuttoned the first two buttons of his shirt. His hair was neat this time and his face looked confident.

“I have asked Ms. Williams to join us for the meeting Mr. Baker, you remember her don’t you?” he indicate for Andrea to take a seat.

The man nodded with a nervous smile in her direction. He was seated in the seat exactly opposite David’s desk and Andrea took the seat a little way from him.

He started complaining about being dragged away from his work and he was a very busy man.

“I appreciate that Mr. Baker but very soon you won’t be so busy,” Michael’s voice was calm and steely.

“What do you mean?” David Baker bristled.

“I mean that you have been embezzling money from the company for years and that ends now because as of now you are no longer working there.”

The man stood up hastily, almost upending the chair he had been sitting on. “How dare you!” he blustered, his face turning red. “I have been working at the company for fifteen years and I have been a very dedicated employee.”

“You have been in debt up to your neck and I am this close to calling the cops Mr. Baker,” Michael said in a steely inflexible voice; rising from his chair as well. “But out of respect for your wife and children I will not be doing so. However if you don’t get your things and leave by the end of the day, I will have to reconsider my position on the matter.”

The man’s shoulders slumped and he sat back down in defeat. “I made some bad business decisions,” he began pleadingly. “I just need another chance, please. I promise never to touch another card again.”

“You’re a compulsive gambler Mr. Baker and you need help; the kind of help I won’t be able to give you. I will write off your debt and I suggest you go home and get the help you need for your wife and children’s sake.”

The man looked as if he was about to protest then with a resigned expression on his face he stood and left the office.

“You handled that well,” Andrea commented.

“You sound surprise,” Michael said with a lifting of one thick brow.

“Just impressed,” Andrea told him with a slight smile.

“I hated having to tell him he had to leave but I had no other choice.” Michael said grimly, leaning back in his chair; his gaze going around the huge office. There were still no changes and the pictures of him and his mother and father were scattered around on every flat surfaces. “He probably would have found a more humane way to deal with the situation.” He murmured.

Andrea looked at him in surprise. “I am not so sure.” She told him gently, his face was unguarded and she saw the sadness portrayed there. “He was a very fair man but he was also a businessman who believed in making sound business decisions and keeping David Baker would have been suicidal.”

“Is that empathy I detect?” he asked turning to look at her in amusement.

“It was and now the moment is over,” she told him dryly, standing with the intention of leaving.

"What is it about me that you don't like?" he asked her suddenly, taking her by surprise. She stood there looking at him; her olive green heels giving her added height and her matching outfit making her look strikingly beautiful and elegant. It struck him suddenly that she was the most beautiful and unattainable woman he had ever seen and he had been around quite a few.

"Everything comes to you easy and you never had to work a day in your life," she told him bluntly. She had probably put her foot in it again but he had asked and she could not help but tell him.

"What if I prove you wrong?" he asked her seriously.

"Why does my opinion of you matter?" she asked him.

"Because we are going to be working together and I would like your opinion of me to change." He answered.

"We'll see," she told him briefly.

"We sure will," he told her mockingly. Andrea had a feeling he was making fun of her and without a word she turned around and left not seeing the speculative expression on his handsome face.

*****

Andrea made a list. She had found that it made sense and she had been using that method since she had started working for Wade Enterprises. It was a list of pros and cons for each company she had been asked to work on.

She was currently working on improving the images of the pharmaceutical company and the hotel that was slated to open in the winter. The hotel was in a very good location and the rooms although shabby now, had excellent structures; it was right in the middle of the business section of town. The interior designers were the best in the business and she was sure that it would look magnificent when it was finished.

She had done up something to be given to the advertising department but she wanted to run it by Michael first before she handed it over.

In the past, she had always worked closely with his father who had jokingly told her that very soon he would have to come to her for advice on what to do because she was very thorough.

It was another late night but she did not mind in the least and she hated going home to an empty apartment sometimes.

She had been in two relationships so far and they had ended in disasters. She was taking it slow these days. The first had been with a banker who, after six months, had told her he wanted to see what else was out there and the other one had felt so genuine that she had allowed herself to care deeply before she found out he had been seeing someone else besides her; now she was single and enjoying it.

*****

Michael looked at the figures with a frown. He had been poring over the financial report for the past half an hour and his brain was getting fuzzy. He was hungry as he had skipped lunch to meet with the financial controller. The man was very good at his job and also very detailed; and for that he was grateful.

He had been so busy he had no time for a personal life and he realized that he did not miss the lifestyle. He had been getting tired of the meaningless round of different women and had a yearning to settle down. The women he had been seeing meant little or nothing to him and he did not see them as people to settle down with.

He pushed the document away from him restlessly and glanced at the watch on his wrist, surprised to see that it was a little after six. He had told Millie to go on home as he had a few things to catch up on.

His cell phone rang and with a wry grimace he realized that it was Diana; his on and off relationship he had been meaning to break off for good; but had not gotten around to doing so.

“Darling, why do I have a feeling you are avoiding me?” her sultry voice had always had the power of making him weak with desire in the past; but now sounded very irritating.

“I told you I have been up to my neck with work Diana,” he told her trying to quell the impatience he was feeling.

“I could come over, I am nearby.” She sounded hopeful.

“It wouldn’t do any of us any good; I have a meeting in a few minutes and it’s going to take some time.” He said quickly. She was a super model who looked good in sack cloth and capitalized on it. Her utter confidence in herself had been one of the reasons he had been attracted to her aside from her beauty but now it just got on his nerves. I must be getting old, he thought wryly.

“Okay darling, I can take a hint.” Diana said with a pout in her voice. “Call me when you are not so busy.”

With promises to call her, he hung up the phone knowing he would not be doing any calling.

He got up from his desk and decided to whip up something for himself in the small private kitchen attached to the office. The chef had already left for the day and he could help himself somewhat.

He made a BLT sandwich and poured himself a tall glass of lemonade and placed it on the marble top counter. He was just about to sit and have the meal when there was a knock on the office door.

“Come on in, I am in the kitchenette,” he called out.

It was Andrea and he felt the sudden shaft of unexplainable pleasure he experienced whenever he saw her. She looked so beautiful and cool that he felt his heart skip a beat.

“I thought I was the only one here,” he commented, beckoning for her to come in.

Andrea glanced at the meal on the counter and looked at him. “There is such a thing as take out,” she told him in amusement. “I am just about to leave but I wanted you to see these first.” She joined him taking a seat on the next stool.

“I am a little tired of take out,” he told her with a grimace, taking the folder from her. Her scent wafted between them and he appreciated the subtle expensive smell. He perused the document in silence and nodded in approval before handing it back to her. “Care to join me?” he asked her.

“Are you going to split the sandwich in two?” she asked in amusement. She did not feel in a hurry to leave.

“I can make one for you,” he was reluctant to see her leave.

“Okay,” she said after a slight hesitation.

“I promised my mother I would stop by tonight for dinner and to check out my old digs. I am planning on moving back home.” He told her as he deftly sliced tomatoes for the sandwich. “I moved out so long ago that it’s going to feel strange to move back there but she is alone in the big house and she needs the company.”

“I am sure she will appreciate it,” she told him politely.

He handed her the sandwich and poured her a glass of lemonade and put them in front of her.

“Any siblings?” he asked her as he took his seat beside her.

Andrea shook her head no. “I am an only child.”

“Me too,” he grinned at her. “I always wanted a sister at least.”

They ate the meal in silence and Michael felt so comfortable around her that he could not believe it.

“I am going to risk getting shut down again by asking you why you are not going home to anyone.” Michael asked her, his eyes holding hers.

Andrea thought about not answering him then with a shrug she said, “I was involved in a relationship with someone and I found out he was with someone else so I decided that it was best to remain single for now.”

“He’s an idiot,” he muttered.

Andrea looked at him in surprise. “I agree with you,” she tilted her head and looked at him, a trace of amusement on her face. “What about you? Or are they too many that you can’t decide which one to get serious with?”

“There goes my lurid reputation again,” he said wryly, pushing away the empty plate. “I am flying solo right now. I guess it’s the heavy responsibility of running a company and besides I was getting tired of the variety.”

He laughed at the expression on her face. “Hard to believe?”

“A little,” she admitted. “I am sure you are going to break quite a few hearts.”

“Is that your way of saying that I am totally irresistible to the opposite sex?” he teased.

“Believe me I find you very easy to resist,” Andrea told him dryly.

“Ouch,” he said rubbing his hand over his heart.

She stood up to leave. “I wish you would stay a little while longer.” He said softly.

"You have already approved the PR information so what else is there for me to stay for?" she asked him puzzled.

"You are very hard on a man's ego aren't you?" he asked her with a wry expression on his face. He had done the usual and folded his shirt up to his forearms; the two top buttons loose.

"If it's ego stroking you need then I am the wrong person," she told him coolly, turning to leave.

"Andrea," his voice stopped her. "Have dinner with me Saturday night."

She turned to look at him in surprise. "You are my boss." She told him stupidly as if that was the only reason.

"So I can order you to go out with me?" he teased her.

"No," she told him shortly. "I don't go out with people I work with and certainly not one I answer to."

"Do you answer to me?" he asked her with a raised brow.

"I do," she told him firmly.

“How about a working dinner?” he persisted. “We could go and check out the progress of the hotel and you can tell me what you think.”

Andrea looked at him for a moment and then she nodded. “As long as you bear in mind that it is a working dinner.” She told him.

He inclined his head and gave her a slight smile "It's a date."

"It's not a date," she reminded him.

He merely smiled at her without answering and she left.

Her scent lingered as if taunting him and in his mind's eye he saw her just before she left his suite of offices in her pencil thin black skirt and her black and white silk blouse. She was unlike any of the other women he was used to and he found himself thinking about her at different times of the day. He saw her sometimes when she was not aware he was looking; having coffee with Millie and laughing at something the other woman said to her and he noticed the way her teeth flashed white against her incredibly beautiful skin.

He was definitely interested and he was determined to break through her reserves.

*****

Gloria dismissed Bertie with a smile. The woman had been with the family for the past twenty years and was more like a family than an employee. They were having dessert in the huge dining room that could easily hold a hundred people. The house was too big and Michael had often wondered why on earth they needed something of this size. His mother who had a degree in interior designing had decorated the house herself. She had gone to many antique road shows and acquired pieces and had them restored.

"How are you doing dear?" she asked her son; giving him a concerned look. He looked relaxed and not in the least bit frazzled.

"Not in the least bit worse for wear," he teased her. She was looking better these days and he knew she had been to the family doctor who was also a long time friend for something to make her sleep better. He told her about the incident with David Baker and casually mentioned that he had asked Andrea Williams, the PRO to sit in on the meeting.

"Your father used to talk about her, said she is very good at what she does." His mother commented.

"Ever met her?" he asked her curiously.

"Several times; beautiful young woman." Gloria looked at her curiously.

"She is quite a woman isn't she?" he said with a laugh as he sipped his cappuccino.

"Is she?" Gloria abandoned her black coffee and gave her son her full attention. She had often hoped and prayed that he would settle down and hoped fervently that when the time came it would not be one of those flighty girls he had been photographed with.

"She does not seem to care that I am the CEO of the company and is totally not impressed with me." He said ruefully.

"Really?" Gloria hid a pleased smile.

"She said that I need to change my image in order for people to take me seriously." Michael told his mother with a twinkle in his eyes.

"Do you agree with her?" she asked him with a teasing smile.

"A little bit," Michael said softly. "I have never met anyone like her."

His mother looked at him in amazement. She had to meet this girl officially; her son sounded like he was smitten or getting there.

She did not make any comment but in her heart she was singing. His father had wished he would settle down and become a part of the company and now it appeared that it was coming to fruition.

*****

Andrea took off her clothes and headed straight for the shower. She had experienced the humidity as soon as she stepped from her car and walked the short distant from the parking garage to her apartment. She had not stopped to think about what he had said to her; she refused to think about it; he was way out of her league and she was not dating anyway. He was probably just looking for a distraction and she fit the bill.

She allowed the warm water to sluice over her body and closed her eyes. She had been disappointed one time too many and she was not about to allow herself to get caught with another handsome face. She was contented and fulfilled with her career and that was enough for now.

Chapter 3

David raised the glass to his lips; his hand shaking badly. He had resort to drinking again since he had been so wrongfully terminated. He had told his wife that he had been given the time off so that the merging of the company could go on and he would be going back in a few weeks to take back his position.

He had been middle management and had been making a lot of money selling drugs from the company and later forced to ship illegal drugs for the people he was in debt to. He had been hesitant at first but they had threatened his family and he'd had to go along with it. He found a way to do so without being caught for a while but he got in over his head and he'd started making mistakes.

Now he no longer had a job thanks to that selfish little boy who thought he ruled the world with all his money that daddy had left him, David thought bitterly. He had his son who was in his final year in college and his daughter just about to go off to college, what was he going to do? He thought in despair.

He emptied the bottle of scotch into the glass and sat there staring at the amber liquid. His wife, Mary Ann had gone to her sister's for the day, along with the kids and he had encouraged them to stay over; it was causing a strain on him; pretending that everything was all right.

He had thought about begging Michael Wade to give him another chance but after he had heard talk about police he'd gotten scared. They were going to lose the house, he thought dispassionately, looking around the den. The house was Mary Ann's pride and joy; a two story modern building he bought the third year he had started working at the pharmaceutical company and now they were going to have to sell it. All because of Michael Wade; he thought bitterly.

*****

"Mr. Wade I did not expect you," Valerie Eddington; the head of the design firm handling the refurbishing of the hotel said agitated. The woman gave Andrea an accusing glance as if it was her fault that Michael Wade; her employer for the biggest account she had, was standing right there in what appeared to be a jumble of mess.

“It’s okay Valerie,” he said smoothly, stepping over a pile of rubble that was once the front parlor. “I always like to see the before and then the after; it impresses me more.”

“We have just started and I showed Ms. Williams the plan already,” the woman was still anxious as if she feared he was going to fire right there on the spot.

Andrea wandered over to where one of the restaurants would be and it was also torn down. Valerie had shown her the design and she had suggested a few changes which had been agreed on.

The woman had expressed concern about it being ready for a winter opening but had said she would put her best men on the job.

Valerie took them on a tour of the entire building and they saw the offices had already been dealt with and would be occupied within the next two weeks. Michael had identified a hotel manager that he would be moving from another hotel they had acquired two years ago.

“Ready for lunch?” he asked Andrea as she made little notes on the pad she had in her hands. He had picked her up at ten and they had headed straight to the hotel. Now, it almost one o'clock.

She nodded.

He spoke briefly to Valerie and the woman apologized again profusely for not getting more done; Michael waved off her apology with a charming smile.

To her surprise they went to a little diner across the street that sold burgers and fries. "I have a weakness for fast food," he told her sheepishly as she watched him biting into the delicious burger. She'd ordered a chicken salad and a pineapple smoothie.

"I would never have guessed," Andrea told him with a smile. He looked like a little boy who had been caught with his hands in the cookie jar. He was dressed in designer jeans and a polo shirt and looked quite unlike the CEO of a multi-billion dollar company. Andrea had worn a long floral skirt and a white sleeveless blouse and had carried a black sweater for when the weather changed as it tended to do in the afternoon.

They ate their meal in companionable silence and Andrea noticed that there was a growing crowd of business people coming and going inside the little restaurant.

“I think the restaurants in the hotel will do a thriving business here,” she commented absently; pulling her smoothie through the straw.

“Can we for one second pretend that I am not the CEO and you are PR and just have a normal lunch?” he asked her teasingly.

“I am not very good at pretending and I did tell you this was not a date,” Andrea said, bringing her attention back to him. His eyes were an incredible shade of green and his lashes were too long to be a male.

“How about a mutual acquaintance having lunch together?” he asked her mildly. He had finished eating and leaned back against the chair; looking at her quizzically.”What do you usually do on a Saturday?”

“Do some housework and then try to come up with new ideas for a particular company I am working on.” Andrea told him, unbending somewhat.

“So basically you are a workaholic,” Michael commented.

She started to deny it but after thinking she answered him, “I never thought of it that way,” she told him thoughtfully. “I always think of it as getting the work done, and time does not matter.”

“So no social life to speak of?” he asked her.

“If you call having lunch with Millie some times; having a social life then that’s about it,” she said ruefully; hearing what it sounded like.

“Want to change that?” he asked her lightly.

“Why when I am having so much fun?” she asked him with a laugh.

“We could hang out sometimes,” he told her.

Andrea looked at him curiously, not taking him seriously. “Of course we can, oh but wait; we don’t move in the same circles do we?”

“I am serious Andrea,” he leaned forward, placing his hands on the table. “I want to take you out on a date.”

“I am not interested Michael; you happen to be my boss,” she told him firmly.

“What if I fired you, would you go out with me then?” he hid a smile at her horrified expression. “Not that I would,” he reassured her. “But apart from me firing you or me resigning from the company how can we solve this dilemma?”

“By you not asking me out again,” Andrea told him; more than a little irritated. “I am sure you are not hard up for female companions; so why not ask one of them.”

“Because I don’t like them the way I like you.” He said with a wry smile.

His admission left her speechless for a minute and Andrea stared at him. He was a little amused and irritated. He was not used to being turned down by women and he was finding it hard not to show his impatience.

“I am flattered you think you like me that way but no thanks,” she told him in a tone of voice that felt as if she was humoring him.

“I am not a damn child Andrea,” he said impatiently. “I am a grown man asking a grown woman to go out with him; it’s not that hard.”

Andrea felt her back going up. “And this grown woman is saying no, so deal with it.” She told him coldly.

They stared at each other for a moment; neither backing down until Michael told her abruptly. “Let’s get you home.”

“Fine by me,” Andrea said coolly.

They traveled to her apartment in silence and he told her a terse goodbye and drove off hastily; leaving her staring after him in irritation. Men! She thought in disgust as she took the elevator to her apartment. The world would be a better place without them.

*****

David did not go straight home. He had packed up his things to move back to his parent’s home but had not entirely given up the apartment. It was his and he liked to be alone sometimes. Now was one of those moments. His mother would probably probe into what had gotten him so rattled. He stared around the almost empty living room that only had a bean bag in the corner and a table in the center of it. The bedroom was still untouched and so was the kitchen. His apartment was nearer to the office building and sometimes when he worked late he felt like just crashing here.

He went into the kitchen and poured himself a stiff drink of whiskey; grimacing as the liquid burned his way down his gut and lit a fire inside him. He missed his father and even though he had spent the latter years jet setting all over the place, they had always been close and he had been able to communicate with him. The weight of the responsibility of running a company so huge was getting to him and sometimes he wondered if he should just let the board run it and go on like he usually did. But he knew he could never go back to that lifestyle. The company was actually growing on him.

He stared down into the liquid broodingly, a slight frown on his brow. So she was not interested in him; big deal. The women he knew would fall all over themselves to spend even a few hours with him but he knew that was one of the reasons why they bored him so easily; they were too accommodating.

He downed the rest of the liquid with distaste; whiskey was never his favorite drink and he had never acquired the taste for it. He was not about to give up on her; he was nothing if not persistent.

*****

Mary Ann was worried about her husband. He had told her everything was fine and he had gotten some vacation leave due to the merging of the company but he was lying and she knew when he was lying. He looked very faraway and unhappy when he thought she was not looking at him and she had heard him whispering on the telephone. She knew he was not cheating on her; he was not the type to do that but something was definitely not right. He had been such a good provider over the years and even though she had insisted that he allowed her to go and work, he had refused, telling her that he was quite capable of taking care of his family. Notwithstanding that she was a trained teacher. She needed to get to the bottom of what was bothering him. She knew it had something to do with the merger but she was not quite sure what. She knew if she asked him outright, she would not get a straight answer.

She'd told her children and her sister and her husband that she had forgotten something at home and she was going to pop on over and come back. The distance was not too great and the several miles were not too taxing. She really needed to get to the bottom of it.

The house was silent even though his car was parked out front. Her begonias were a little wilted, she thought absently. She took great pride in her garden and spent many days during the summer pruning and weeding because it relaxed her and she loved that her garden was the show piece in the neighborhood.

She found him in the den slumped over the desk and an empty bottle of scotch beside him. For a minute she thought the worse had happened and she ran the rest of the way and shook him hard, her heart beating hard.

“David!” she shouted when he did not respond. “David wake up!” To her immense relief he felt warm, so he was not dead.

He stirred and looked up at her; his eyes blurry and bloodshot. “Mary Ann?” his voice was slurred and Mary Ann took in his disheveled appearance. He had not changed his clothes since they had left this morning. “Where are the children?”

"Back at my sister's place," she told him impatiently. "Why are you drinking?"

"I had a little too much to drink, no big deal," he tried to smile but failed dismally.

"What's wrong?"

"Nothing," he tried standing but stumbled and almost fell.

"What's going on David?" she asked him firmly, guiding his faltering steps to the couch and sitting beside him. "And don't tell me that everything is fine. We have been married for too long for me not to know when everything is certainly not fine."

She was alarmed when she saw him slumped over with a look of defeat on his face.

"I made a fine mess of things," he made a weak attempt at smiling. "I lost my job. That miserable son of a gun Wade fired me."

Mary Ann stared at her husband as if she was seeing him for the first time. She should have seen the signs and if she had not been too caught up in the flower show she had been preparing for in the past several weeks she would have seen it.

"What happened?" she asked him quietly. Whatever it was they would fix it and if it meant that she would have to go out and look for something to do; it was going to be okay.

"I owed the company money." He told her dejectedly; telling her how he had gambling debts and he was in over his head. He told her everything and she listened; not saying a word even though her heart felt as if it was exploding out of her body.

"You need to start taking responsibilities for your actions and stop blaming Mr. Wade for your problems David," she told him quietly, even though she felt like smacking him all the way to the next state. How could he have been so stupid and selfish?

"He didn't have to fire me," he protested and Mary Ann gave him a quelling glance. "I am going to fix this Mary Ann," he told her feverishly.

"We are going to fix this David," she amended firmly; she had no idea how it was going to be done but it had to; they had the children to think about.

*****

"How about this?" Andrea showed him the document she had revised. They were in her office and to her relief, he'd not mentioned the disastrous lunch they'd had together a week ago. He had been in and out of the building for the past few days dealing with another merger and she had barely caught a glimpse of him. Maybe he had gotten her out of his system; she thought and tried to tell herself that it was a good thing.

He read it and passed it back to her with a small notation for her to change something. He was dressed in a blue dress shirt and rolled up the sleeves as was his usual practice and he was leaning over her desk.

"How have you been?" he asked her.

"Okay, how about you?" she asked him politely.

"Very well," he said equally polite.

"That's good," she nodded.

"I can't do this," he told her abruptly, moving away. It was almost five o'clock and several of the staff had already left.

"What do you mean?" she asked him puzzled; staring up at him.

"Trying to pretend we are just employer and employee and doing this polite dance with you," he told her impatiently.

"Michael-" she began and he stopped her.

"I don't want to hear it Andrea," he said running agitated fingers through his dark hair. "I am attracted to you and want to take it further, so please stop telling me that it won't work."

"It won't," she told him quietly, settling back against her chair. "I am not going out with you, so you need to stop."

"I am not going to stop," he told her forcefully.

They stared at each other and Andrea felt the attraction between them but she was not going to let it get the better of her. She had worked too hard to reach where she was and she was not going to let her libido make her lose everything.

He left without saying another word and Andrea slumped into her seat with relief. He was starting to wear down her resistance.

*****

Andrea went home early for a change. She had secretly feared that he would come back to her office and take up where they left off and he was starting to get to her.

She had picked up a few things at the supermarket and decided to prepare herself something to eat. Her kitchen was spotless and hardly used as she did not relish eating alone and she did not have much tolerance for preparing a meal. She was hardly ever home and when she was she ordered take out.

Michael Wade had gotten to her and she was irritated by him. She had been doing so well on her own; enjoying her job and the challenges it posed and had been contented with being single until he had started making her aware of herself as a woman. Damn him. She thought in irritation. He was out of her league and she was not going to date her employer; no matter how handsome and persuasive he was.

Her phone rang just as she was about to put the pasta to boil. For one minute she thought it was him calling her but she saw that it was Millie. She had left before her at work and had not gotten the chance to talk to her today.

"You ran off so fast today what happened?" she demanded.

"Something has to be wrong for me to leave early and come home for once?" Andrea asked her.

"Yes," Millie answered promptly. "You practically live at that place so for you to leave early; it means that something is wrong."

"I was tired and decided to come home and get some rest." Andrea said evasively.

"Are you sure?" Millie persisted.

"Yes, mother," Andrea said patiently. "Don't you have a husband and child to tend to?"

"Mark is in his study with his head buried in marking papers and Simone is on her lap top so I am basically alone." Millie said dryly.

"Poor Millie," Andrea said with a laugh.

She sniffed and then said; "Our esteemed employer is not so bad after all."

"I am beginning to think that way also," Andrea said casually. She had contemplated telling Millie what Michael had said to her but decided against it.

"Some members of the board are not too pleased with his performance; they were expecting him to fail drastically so that they would be able to pick up the pieces."

"I guess he is proving them wrong," Andrea said in amusement.

"He is;" Millie said with a laugh. "I am rooting for him; too handsome for my purpose, I much them prefer them plain like my dear Mark," she said with a grin.

Andrea laughed because she knew first hand that her husband was a strapping handsome man who adored her.

"When are you going to find a man to go out with and stop working so hard?" Andrea wondered if it was a conspiracy.

"I am quite fine the way I am," she told her friend firmly.

"Mark has this lovely man at school that would be just right for you, I am having an end of summer barbecue next Saturday and he will be here."

"Don't you dare!" Andrea said laughingly. "I am not interested in being set up with some man I don't even know."

"You need to get out there," Millie protested.

"Goodbye Millie," she told the girl firmly.

"Think about it," her friend told her before hanging up.

Andrea shook her head and went back inside the kitchen to finish preparing her dinner.

Chapter 4

“This is not acceptable Michael,” Andrea stormed into his office; hurrying past a startled Millie and pushing the door open. He was on the phone and she just did not care; she was furious. It had been a week now since he had told her that he was not giving up on her. He had not called her or even said anything else to her and she had told herself that she did not care.

“Close the door,” he told her calmly; hanging up the phone.

“I prefer to leave it open,” Andrea stood in the center of the room; her eyes flashing. “You took the designers off the hotel job and sent them elsewhere Michael; we have a deadline that we are scarcely able to meet as it is.”

He walked past her to close the door. Taking her arm, he led her to one of the chairs in front of his desk. “I did what I think is prudent,” he told her, going to the side table to pour some water in a glass and handed it to her.

Andrea stared at him in frustration and then with an impatient sigh she took the glass from him. “You did not have the decency to pick up the phone and talk to me about it? This is a PR's nightmare Michael."

"An excellent PR like you will know how to spin it," he told her smoothly. "I have faith in you."

She looked at him in frustrated anger and he just stared back at her; his eyebrows raised in question. "You're making my job more difficult," she told him with a frown.

"And you're making being around you and not getting an answer from you incredibly frustrating Andrea," he told her.

She felt her heart stutter inside her chest and she did not know how to respond. "Michael," she lifted her hand in protest, and then she let it drop back down.

"I need you to start working on salvaging the image of the pharmaceutical company," he told her; his attention going back to the urgent matter on hand. He had spent the last few nights digging into the damage done by David Baker and several other employees and was furious at how much damage had been caused. He had felt like going right over to the Baker's house and wringing the man's neck.

It was then that Andrea saw it. The utter weariness on his handsome face. His hair looked as if he had been raking his fingers through it all morning. She felt her heart go out to him; his job was not easy and she had barged into his office and piled on more frustration than he was already facing. It was a wonder he did not have her thrown out.

"I will do my best," she told him quietly; her way of telling him that she was sorry.

He looked at her in surprise at her mellow tone. "Good," he said briskly. "I will see what you have for later." He told her.

Andrea stood up to leave. "You're doing a good job," she told him quietly as she headed for the door.

"Was that a compliment I heard?" he asked; a smile tilting the side of his lips.

"Take it for what it is, you won't be getting many more of those," she told him dryly before leaving the office.

Michael stared after her; watching the gentle sway of her hips in a gray wool skirt she had on; as usual, her tantalizing scent was left in the office long after she had departed. He had decided to give her some time and in the meantime he had been distracted by what he had found out in the pharmaceutical company. His social life had gone to pieces and was going to have to do something about it fast.

*****

David Baker hid the gun in his pouch. He had thought about it carefully and even though he had pretended to his wife that he was picking up the pieces of his life; he was not doing so. He went to bed every night and as soon as he knew she was sleeping he would get out of the bed quietly and creep into the study to some online gambling. Now he was in debt again and his debtors were demanding payment or else. Mary Ann had gone ahead and taken a job at the local school and had reassured him they would be all right but he was not so sure about that. It was all Michael Wade's fault and that snotty PR woman who had been sitting in on the meeting and hearing every humiliating thing that had been said to him. He was brought down low and he did not know how to get back up. He smiled sadly as he thought about his wife; they had had so many dreams and had been so in love when they were younger. He was still in love with her; she had not judged him or even blamed him for the mess he had put them in and for that, he respected her so much but he could not afford for her to be hurt or disgraced.

He had done all the right things but he had seen the furtive looks his children had given him. He was afraid the respect was gone and he was never going to get it back. He was used to a certain lifestyle and he did not know how to cope without it.

It was a Friday evening. He remembered evenings like this when he had sat there in his office and had a drink for the road or if he was going to be gambling, he would tell Mary Ann he was going for a drink with the guys. Now he had no friends because they had disappeared when he got fired; so much for that.

He had told the guard at the door that he had an appointment with Mr. Wade and had even flashed his work id that they had not bothered to ask him to turn in. Who was the fool now, he thought grimly as he rode the elevator up to the top floor. It was a little after seven but he knew they were still at work because he had been watching behind a palm tree to see who was coming from the building and they had not surfaced. He had told Mary Ann he was going to take a walk and he would be right back. He had dug himself in so deep a hole that he did not know how to come out of it.

He gazed at the expensive art work on the wall and wondered briefly if he should just try to fence some of them but he shook his head; he was not a petty thief after all.

He reached her door first and he stood there staring into her office. She had her head bent over something. She was writing and was not even aware of the threat of danger just lurking outside her door. He looked around quickly and noticing that there was no one around he approached the office and stepped inside.

“Michael I am not finished yet I-“ she looked up and the rest of the sentence fizzled off as she realized who it was. “Mr. Baker; how may I help you?”

“I am not so sure Ms. Williams,” he pulled the gun from the pouch; and aimed it at her. “It is Ms Williams isn’t it?”

Andrea felt her heart stop and her mouth went dry. She knew Michael was somewhere in the building but she was not sure who else was around. He was way too calm and that was very dangerous.

She had a panic buzzer under her desk but she was afraid of moving her hands in case he saw her and started shooting. She had to keep him occupied somehow.

“Mr. Baker I am sure whatever it is we can work something out,” she forced herself to remain calm and to stop her hands from trembling. Where was everyone? She thought in despair.

“Can we?” he came further into the room; the hand holding the gun steady. “Can you get me my job back? Can you send my children to school and make sure my family will be all right financially? If there is a chance you can do that Ms. Williams I am willing to hear you out.”

She seized upon the meat of the matter; his family! “I am sure your family would not approve of what you are thinking of doing Mr. Baker; nothing is worth what you’re planning on doing.”

“Leave my family out of it!” he shouted, his hand trembling slightly and Andrea knew she had hit a nerve. “My family is suffering because I was unfairly dumped after I had put in fifteen years of faithful service and now it’s time to get justice for what has been done to me and my family.”

Her eyes widened slightly as she noticed that Michael had run in to see what the commotion was about. He stood stock still for a moment; his hands clenched into fists as he realized what was going on.

With a deliberate movement she swiftly turned her eyes back to the nearly demented man standing in front of her. He can't know that Michael was standing behind him; God knows what he would do. She hoped fervently that Michael had the presence of mind to go and get help and not play the hero.

"Mr. Baker-" she began and he shouted, "Shut up!" waving the gun at her; his eyes bulging and his teeth bared in anger. "No more talking! I don't want to talk do you hear me? I don't care anymore so I don't want to hear anything else from you. You people ruined my life and I can't - I don't know what to do anymore!" his voice had gone down to a pitiable whimper and there were tears in his eyes.

By this time Michael had come back and with him were several guards. Andrea shook her head at them.

"What are you doing?" he demanded, noticing that her attention was not on him. He spun around and saw that they had company and ran into the corner of the room; his gun still trained on her. "Tell my wife I am sorry." He murmured.

Without another word he put the gun to his head and fired a shot; slumping to the floor as Andrea's scream rent the room. The men rushed in then and Michael ran towards her, pulling her into his arms; his heart thumping furiously.

He pulled her out of the room as the paramedics and the police who had been called earlier crowded into her office. Michael held her shaking body close to his as he took a seat and pulled her onto his lap stroking her back as he tried to comfort her.

She vaguely heard when a detective came over to ask some questions and Michael told him that he would deal with it later. She wanted to bury herself in his arms and forget the horror that had unfolded inside her office a few minutes ago. A man had blown his brains out right before her and she could not help but be thankful that it had been him and not her.

It was half an hour before she could stir herself to pull away from him but he held her still. "Are you up to answering some questions from the detectives?" he asked her gently, lifting her chin to stare at her in concern.

She nodded.

He made an indication to the detectives in charge and standing, he went with her inside the board room with the two detectives. Andrea answered their questions automatically; grateful for Michael's support and the hand he placed on her shoulder.

They wanted to know what she knew about David Baker and why he had targeted her in the first place. Michael told them about the ongoing investigation from his P.I. Company on the former employees of the pharmaceutical company they had acquired before his father's death and how they had had to let go of Mr. Baker because of his illegal activities.

The detectives left shortly after and told them that the office was considered a crime scene so it should not be used until further notice.

"I have all my documents in there, what should I do?" Andrea asked them.

"I will ask the crime scene personnel when you can go and get your stuff right now Ms. Williams," Detective Farrady said politely. He put away his note pad and gave her a reassuring smile. “I know you have been through a terrible ordeal so I would advise you to go home and see if you can get some rest.”

“I will see to it that she get home safe Detective,” Michael told him; squeezing her shoulder gently. “Please keep me posted as to the development.”

“You’re coming home with me,” he told her firmly as they stood up to leave. The detectives had already left and the crime scene persons were already packing up their equipment to leave as well.

“Andrea please,” he said wearily as she was about to protest. “I will sleep better knowing I can see you.”

“All right fine,” she said ungraciously. Her documents and the things she had been working on were already taken out by the men and placed in an empty office across from Michael’s. It was to be her temporary office for now.

Andrea avoided looking into her office as if by doing so she could forget what had happened there. Michael placed her inside his car and she settled back against the soft upholstery with a weary sigh; her mind flashing back to what had happened and how close she had come to losing her own life.

“Take your mind off it,” he advised her as he put the car into drive and moved away from the curb.

“How do you suggest I do that?” she asked him, her voice riddled with despair. “He had a family Michael and he just threw that away without thought of what this was going to do to them. What’s going to happen to them?”

“I promise you I will try and sort it out,” he told her briefly, his mouth tightening. “Baker was in way over his head Andrea. He had started gambling again and he had done more damage that we had first found out. You’re going to have to show yourself to be one hell of a PR to get the company out of the hole it is in.”

“You don’t feel sorry for him do you?” she asked him curiously; noting the grim expression on his face.

“I feel sorry for his family but I have no tolerance for men like that who think you are supposed to feel sorry for them because you owe them something.” He said, his hands tightening on the steering wheel.

They had reached his apartment building by then and he drove in the underground parking lot to park the car. They went up to the building in silence and Andrea could not help but wonder how many other women he had brought inside.

He called his mother and explained the situation to her. Andrea called Millie and told her about it.

“How about some brandy?” he asked her, going over to the liquor cabinet.

“No,” she told him wrinkling her pretty nose.

“It’s a sure fire medicine for getting over shock.” He told her teasingly.

“No thank you,” she told him dryly. “What happened to the furniture?” she asked him curiously, staring around the almost bare room.

“I am not really living here,” he told her; downing the brandy in one gulp. “I only come here when I work too late to go home to the family home. Want something to eat?”

“I am not hungry,” she told him listlessly. She settled back on the single couch that was in the room. “I keep thinking there was something I could have done." She said despairingly. He came over and pulled her up and sat down, putting her on his lap.

"There was nothing you could do Andrea," he told her firmly. "I thought I would die when I saw him standing there pointing that gun at you; I couldn't move, couldn't function and for a minute, I wanted to run in there and tear his head off," his voice was harsh and the hands holding her tightened around her waist.

Andrea felt touched by his passionate admission.

"I was afraid," she told him, her head buried on his shoulder. "I was so scared Michael that I did not know what to do. I thought I was going to die."

He held her close to him; his thoughts flashing back to the moment he had seen her with the gun pointed at her. He had never felt so scared in all his life at the thought of losing her and he realized without a shadow of a doubt, that he wanted no one else but her; he just had to make her realize it as well.

She fell asleep in his arms and he gently lifted her and took her to the bedroom. She had taken off her shoes and with a slight hesitation he took off her shirt and found a warm blanket to cover her with. He did not trust himself to sleep beside her so he settled himself on the sofa that was in the room.

Andrea dreamed that she was in the office and she was trapped in the room with David Baker. He was running her all over the room waving a gun at her and telling her that she was responsible for all his troubles. No matter how fast she ran he was catching up with her and just as he was about to hold on to her, she jumped out of her sleep with a scream rising from her throat.

Michael jumped up as he heard her scream and ran towards her, gathering her shaking body into his arms. She held on to him tightly as she tried to control the terror inside her.

“It’s okay baby,” he said soothingly, pulling her closer to him. “It’s okay; it was just a bad dream.”

They slept in each other’s arms for the remainder of the night and even when she had fallen asleep, he was still awake. Her being in his arms was not doing very well for him. He smiled to himself wryly; this was certainly a first for him – having a woman in his arms that he was fiercely attracted to and not doing anything about it.

She felt so vulnerable. He wanted to be the hero and protect her from all the bad things in the world – he wanted to be her champion. He knew if she ever dreamed he was thinking of her as a helpless damsel in distress she would have his head. She had come into his life and turned it around without even trying and without even being aware of it. He no longer felt the need to go out with other women and he wondered what his acquaintances would think of him now. He needed only her and she was giving him a warm time with rich boy and employer crap.

He sighed and pulled her closer to him as he drifted off to sleep; she felt right in his arms and he fell asleep with a smile on his lips.

Chapter 5

The fall out was huge. The headlines screamed: "Man committed suicide after being fired by new head of Wade Enterprises" and in smaller print it went on to reveal all the frivolous lifestyle of playboy Michael Wade and subtly suggested he was not qualified to follow in his father's footsteps.

Michael was furious. He had been pacing in his office like a caged tiger for the past hour and had been snapping at anyone who came near him. The board had called a meeting to discuss the method they should use to deal with the matter. To make matters worse; the paper had interviewed David's wife and children and sympathy was leaning towards them.

"Andrea get in here!" he said, abruptly calling her on the intercom. She stiffened with outrage and was about to tell him a piece of her mind when she decided against it.

Since she had spent the night at his house and had left the next morning without saying a word, he had been on edge and to come Monday morning to encounter this crisis was too much.

Millie looked at her sympathetically as she hurried past her and went into his office. He looked so haggard. She wanted to go over and take him into her arms but she had a feeling he would not appreciate it.

“What are we going to do about this?” he asked abruptly, barely sparing her a glance as he slapped the newspaper in front of her.

“I have already called the newspaper to do an interview and you need to make a statement,” she told him calmly, taking a seat without being told to do so. “Tell the story without making David into a monster; that will only make it worse. I am planning to tell them my ordeal when he held a gun at me and how scared I was for my life.”

He heaved a sigh and rested against the desk. “I am being judged by my lifestyle which should not be anyone’s business,” he said grimly. “If that miserable man was still alive I would wring his neck without a second thought.”

“Make sure you get out of that mind frame before you face the press,” Andrea warned him; even though she was agreeing with him secretly. “It will pass, another big story will let it disappear and the company has too much credibility to fall.”

"How are you?" he asked her changing the subject suddenly. He had not shaven and he rubbed the growth of beard on his jaw reflectively.

"I am okay," she told him. "Thanks for being there for me."

"No problem," he told her wryly. "Tell Millie I am ready for the sharks now."

Andrea stood and made to leave. "Andrea we have unfinished business."

She turned back to look at him and seeing the look of determination on his handsome face she nodded and left the room.

"He's ready for the board," she told Millie stopping briefly at her friend's desk.

"How are you?" Millie asked in concern.

"Hanging in there," Andrea said truthfully.

"He doesn't deserve the backlash," Millie said shaking her blond head.

“He doesn’t,” Andrea agreed. The phone rang just then and Andrea waved at her and left. Her office was still a crime scene even though the yellow tape had been removed and even so Andrea did not feel she could go back in there any time soon.

She slumped in the chair and rested her head into her hands and took several deep breaths. The truth was she had not been sleeping well the past two nights and the nightmare kept coming back but she did not want to burden Michael with her problem. She had to admit sleeping in his arms that night had felt so good, she wanted to repeat it but she was not going to get involved with someone again and discover it was a mistake. He was her employer and she would not be able to recover from it. She loved her job too much.

She stared at the statement she had been doing up and reaching for the phone she punched in a number. She had a contact at a rival newspaper and she intended to use it to fix the problem.

*****

Gloria came for the board meeting. Usually she stayed away from the business aspect, preferring to let the men do their thing; knowing full well that as much as they were living in a progressive era; men did not take too kindly to women venturing into what they called their territory. But this was different; she was a member of the board and her son needed her for moral support. She was not about to let a bunch of stiff necked elderly men deprive her of taking her rightful place in the board room. Her husband would have wanted it that way. Besides she wanted to officially meet the girl who had Michael tied up in knots.

That awful man had caused a lot of problems and she was glad that both her son and Andrea were none the worse for wear. She had dressed in a chic lemon suit and her blonde hair was elegantly swept on top of her head. She knew she still turned heads when she went anywhere and today was no exception as she swept into the room. The men stood up politely as she made her way towards the head of the large table. Michael taking the seat beside her. "Please be seated gentlemen and let's see what can be done." She said her tone barely civil. "We have a crisis on our hand that was caused by a man who was greedy and foolish enough to think he could play with fire and not get burnt. As a board, I expect us to bond together and quell the nasty rumors going around about Michael's inability to run the company his father left in his care. My husband was not a fool and he would not have left the company to his son if he knew he would run it to the ground, no matter how much he loved him. I expect we are all going to rally around the CEO of this company that has given us the opportunity to live like we do." There was a hushed silence around the room and everybody nodded slowly in agreement; some rather reluctantly but did not dare voice any opposition.

The meeting went on without any further hitch and the decision was made to go along with the damage control.

*****

Gloria left the meeting early, leaving the men to discuss matters that were boring her to death and went to find the charming beautiful girl that had her son wrapped up in confusion. She found her in the office adjoining her son's and her eyebrows quirked in amusement as she realized that it had being a deliberate movement on her son's part to keep her near to him as there were several empty offices she could have used.

"My dear, I hate to interrupt as you seem so hard at work," she said from the open doorway, her quick eyes noticing the girl's dark red skirt suit that suited her so well and her short cropped hair that framed a face of magnificent beauty. She did not have to try to stand out, she already did.

“Mrs. Wade, I didn’t hear you come in,” Andrea felt a little intimated by the woman’s cool beauty and her extreme confidence.

“Of course you didn’t,” Gloria came further inside the office, glancing at the notes she had been writing on her notepad. “You were busy coming up with ways to defray the damage that has been done to the company by that awful incident. How are you?”

Andrea was a little distressed when the woman took a seat. “I am getting there,” she said politely.

“Oh my dear, please don’t stand on ceremony where I am concerned” she said with a gay laugh, waving an elegant hand. “I am just a concerned mother right now, making sure my son and the company my husband worked so hard to build is going to be okay.”

“I am sure everything will blow over without too much damage,” Andrea reassured her; going back around her desk.

“I have made a call to a rival newspaper and they are going to print an entire different story, the truth.”

“I am sure you are very good at your job my dear; I have every confidence in your ability,” Gloria told her. “I just wanted to meet you in person, I have heard so much about you.”

Andrea looked at her startled as if she had dropped a bomb in her lap and Gloria hid her smile.

“I am not sure what you heard,” Andrea said uncertainly,

“All good things my dear,” Gloria said standing up, ready to take her leave. “A pleasure to finally meet you my dear.” And with a smile she was gone; leaving the expensive smell of her perfume in the office and Andrea staring after her uncertainly.

*****

Michael made a statement to the press and the papers printed a retraction. They were going ahead with the merger and the pharmaceutical company was going to up and running by the next two weeks.

They were in the office fine tuning the latest statement on the company. It was after seven in the evening and the rest of the staff had already left. The security had been tightened up since the incident a week ago and Michael had ordered up dinner for them to eat while they work.

"I want to cook dinner for you this weekend," he said suddenly as he made a change on the document she had handed him. It was Thursday and they had several documents spread on the soft comfortable couch between them. Andrea had taken off her black heels and was in her stocking feet.

"You cook?" she looked at him in amazement.

"I cook," he told her in amusement. He had pulled up his shirt sleeves like he normally did and his face looked relaxed and quite unlike the harried look he had worn over the past few days.

"You are not going to give up are you?" Andrea asked with a sigh, secretly glad that he was still interested and he had not forgotten about her.

"Not a chance," he told her promptly. "I am very interested and besides if you save someone's life; that life automatically belongs to you."

“When did you save my life?” she asked him tilting her head to one side.

“How quickly we forget,” he teased, reaching out to pull her into his arms, disregarding the papers he crushed in his attempt to get her close to him.

“Michael,” she protested as he pulled her into his arms. “We have work to do.”

“It can wait,” he told her softly. “All work and no play make us dull people.” He murmured.

There was silence for a few minutes as they shared a passionate kiss. Michael refused to let her go after and Andrea was reluctant to move out of his arms.

*****

The dinner was grilled chicken and sweet potato salad. He refused to let her help him; giving her a glass of white wine and letting her sit on one of the stools by the beautiful granite counter and watch him cook. He certainly knew his way around the kitchen, she thought in surprise.

"I never dreamed a person like you could tell one part of the stove from the next," she commented as she watched him stir the potatoes on the stove top.

"A person like me?" he asked his brows rose.

"Wealthy and don't have to go into the kitchen." Andrea teased.

"Now who's doing the stereotyping?" he said dryly. "Mom believed in me being well rounded; she is always saying that no amount of money could bail you out of a situation where you find yourself with no supermarkets or take out around and you have to prepare something for yourself."

"Smart woman," Andrea said in admiration. "Speaking of which: what have you been telling her about me?"

"What makes you think I have been telling her about you?" he said evasively.

"Because she told me she had heard so much about me," Andrea told him.

"I just mentioned how good you are at your job, that's all," he said with a shrug, turning back to the stove.

“Really?” she said looking at him skeptically.

“Fishing for compliments?” he asked her in amusement. She was wearing blue denims and a pink sweater and her face was devoid of make-up which made her look like an adorable teenager.

“Absolutely not,” she told him with a slight smile. “I don’t have to fish.”

“Cocky,” he grinned.

They had dinner in the kitchen shortly after and it was quite delicious. He told her about growing up as a child and even though he had all the opportunities available to him; his father especially made sure that he knew other people had a difficult time growing up so he should always be aware that they had a lot to give thanks for.

Andrea told him about growing up without her parents and how hard it was and still is when she thought about it.

They had dessert. Chocolate mousse he had ordered from a delicatessen that was famous for making delicious pastries.

Andrea felt relaxed and comfortable in his presence and she realized she was letting down her reserves.

“I am falling in love with you Andrea,” he told her suddenly. They had finished eating and he had spread a huge towel against the fireplace and she was lying on his chest; very sleepy and relaxed. His statement brought her upright instantly and she rose on her elbow to look into his green eyes.

“You don’t mean that,” she told him firmly.

“I am old enough to know and say what I mean,” he told her dryly.

“Michael, we have been thrown together for some time and we went through a horrible tragedy where a man took his life right in front of us so that’s maybe what you’re experiencing now.” She was agitated.

“Thanks for making me appear like a complete imbecile,” he said sitting up abruptly. “I am falling in love with you and this has been going on for some time now so don’t tell that it was because of what happened, I am not an imbecile Andrea.”

“I am sorry Michael,” She said contritely, reaching out a hand to touch his rigid arm. “This is a shock to me and I don’t know how to handle it. I had been in two relationships that went pretty bad and I swore I would not let it happen to me again.”

“So you have sworn off love?” he quizzed.

“No,” she shook her head; her expression pensive.

“I am falling in love with you,” he told her firmly. “I know what I feel and I have been feeling that way for quite some time. I don’t want to be with anyone else but you Andrea so deal with it.” He pulled her into his arms and spent a significant amount of time showing her how much.

*****

“I don’t know what to do about it Millie,” Andrea told her friend. They were having lunch after escaping from the office. She had told Michael she was having lunch with Millie and he had wanted to know if she would be coming over to his place later; she had told him yes. “I am used to him being a playboy and I am scared that I will get involved with him and discover he has not changed.”

“Michael Wade in love with you!” Millie shook her blonde head in wonder as she spooned the chicken soup into her mouth. “Oh the mighty have fallen.”

“You’re not helping Millie,” Andrea reproved her friend. She was feeling a little restless and she wondered why she was feeling so muddled. She had spent the night at his place and she had not wanted to go home the next day. He had wanted her to stay as well but she had gone home. Not that it had made any difference any way because she had spent the day thinking about him and the way he made her feel.

“Honey, I am sure he is telling you the truth, he has not been with anyone since he took over the running of the firm; so I am sure that his being so hard at work is the only reason.” Millie told her seriously. “He’s quite a catch; a lot of women would kill to be in your place.”

“That’s what I am afraid of,” Andrea said seriously. “He is so used to women falling all over themselves that he will probably expect me to do the same.”

“Come on Andrea, you know that you don’t suffer fools gladly and Michael is well aware that he cannot play those games with you.” Millie reminded her.

“I don’t know how I feel about him,” Andrea pushed aside the burger she had been eating; her appetite suddenly nonexistent. “But I know when I am not with him that I wish I were.”

“Sounds like love to me,” Millie commented; looking at her friend speculatively. “Look honey, I know you have been hurt twice before but you cannot let that stop you from experiencing true love; you would be losing out on a lot.”

“I know,” Andrea said with a sigh. “But Michael Wade? I am just a simple person and I am not used to being in the limelight and having my life under the camera; I don’t think I can deal with it.”

“Talk to him about it and tell him how you feel,” Millie told her gently.

*****

Michael was well aware that the crisis was far from over. Even though the board had been doing its best to show a measure of support, he knew they were still looking for him to make the slightest slip so they could show they had been right all along. He knew that no matter what he did to prove himself it would never be enough for the stodgy stuff shirts that made up the board. He had decided to use another tack; no longer was he going to be looking for approval – he was in charge and he was going to start letting them know he was the one in charge.

Andrea came in just as he had finished talking to the decorators. “Perfect timing,” he told her; admiring her rose pink pants suit and the way the fabric molded to her shapely curves.”I just spoke to Valerie and it appears we are going to be ahead of schedule for the pharmaceutical company.”

“That’s great,” Andrea said, her eyes lighting up. “I just need to get some details from her and then send out a press release.”

“Good,” he nodded, a little distracted.

“What’s wrong?” she asked him.

“What makes you think that something is wrong?” he asked her lightly.

“Stop playing games Michael, something is wrong.” Andrea said impatiently. He was standing behind his desk and shifting around some papers.

With a sigh he showed her the headline. It was yesterday's paper and there was a big picture of him with a striking blonde hanging on to his arm and the headline screamed: 'Playboy Michael Wade with fiancé supermodel Diana Wellington'.

Andrea put the paper back down and looked at him silently.

"I was engaged to her several years ago and I broke it off when I found out that it was not working out. She called me yesterday and wanted to come over. I told her I was seeing someone else so I guess this is her idea of payback." He told her quietly trying to gauge her reaction, she was too calm. He had wanted to wring Diana's neck when he saw the headline. She had friends in the media and she had always used her beauty to get results.

"Say something," he insisted quietly.

"This is neither the time nor the place," Andrea told him coolly and from her tone he knew he was going to be in for a hard time.

"Andrea please; tell me at least that you understand and it does not affect what we have." He pleaded.

“What do we have exactly Michael?” she asked him, her heart tearing in pieces with jealousy and she hated herself for it. The girl was incredibly beautiful and if she should stand beside her she would go unnoticed, she thought in despair.

“Don’t you dare compare yourself to her,” he came from around his desk and stood in front of her; he wanted to touch her but he did not dare. “You are the most beautiful and talented woman I have ever known and I want you to believe that.”

“I have work to do,” she muttered backing away with the intention of fleeing. He held her arm and stopped her.

“Please don’t leave like this Andrea,” he said hoarsely, actually feeling the fear invade his heart. He could not lose her, not for something like this.

“We’ll talk about it later,” she told him; not sure she wanted to.

He hesitated, still holding on to her before releasing her. He had to believe that she was going to listen to what he had to say.

She went back to her office and try as she might, she could not concentrate on what she had to do. He had been engaged and he had not told her about it. They had talked about so many different things and yet he had conveniently not remembered to tell her about that part of his life.

Her phone rang just then and to her surprise it was Gloria. "I was told to call and do damage control." Gloria's amused voice came over the phone.

"Mrs. Wade!" Andrea said in surprise.

"Gloria dear," the woman said kindly. "My son is having a conniption fit over that nonsensical article because he believes that it's going to cause him in what he termed as the most important relationship in his life."

"Mrs. Wade – Gloria," Andrea amended; silently berating Michael. "I don't know what Michael told you but I told him we would discuss it later."

"He is very concerned my dear and for my son to call me to intervene then I would say it is very important to him." Gloria said mildly. "Diana Wellington was a taker and a very shallow person. She wanted to advance her career and she used

Michael to do so but thank God he realized early enough what she was up to and ran for his life. She is only surface my dear with no depth at all. You have nothing to worry about."

"Thanks Gloria," she said quietly, her heart settling. "I am glad you called."

"No problem my dear and please tell that son of mine I would like him to bring you around for dinner very soon; we really should get to know each other better."

They said goodbye and hung up the phone. Andrea sat there looking at the phone in bemusement and wondered about the course her life was taking.

Chapter 6

The relationship was tentative at least on Andrea's part. He had been trying to prove to her that he was a changed person but still she was cautious. They had been going out for the past three months and they were supposed to be celebrating their three month anniversary. He was planning to take her to a very fancy restaurant. Andrea was just putting on her make-up when the dizzy spell came over her. She frowned thoughtfully as she closed her eyes trying to get her bearings back. Maybe it was due to the fact that she had skipped lunch because her appetite had been nonexistent from the other day.

He picked her up a little after seven wearing suit pants and a blue silk shirt. She was wearing a black dress that molded her figure to perfection.

"Hey," he kissed her softly on the mouth; his lips lingering before opening the passenger side of the car for her to get in.

They had gone to his mother's for dinner and she had been sufficiently impressed by the size and luxury of the place when she had been taken on a tour by Gloria. They had spent the evening chatting pleasantly with Gloria hinting around at marriage.

Michael had also mentioned it to her tentatively and she had told him she was not ready to think about that yet; they should just take it slow for the time being. He was frustrated but he tried to be patient for her benefit.

They were shown to a coveted seat in the corner and away from the crowd. She spotted several celebrities and tried not to appear to be staring. “Come here often?” she asked him teasingly. She was beginning to feel lightheaded again but chalked it down to her lack of eating.

“Not much,” he answered her seriously. She looked so breathtaking that he only had eyes for her. He had asked her several times to be his wife and she had told him she was not ready. “You’re so beautiful,” he murmured, reaching for her hand across the table.

“Thanks, you don’t look so bad yourself.” She smiled at him. She knew what she was feeling for him but she was determined not to jump into anything too soon. He looked so handsome, she could not believe he only wanted to be with her.

They came with the food, lobster in lemon sauce and a delicate shrimp broth. Suddenly and without warning Andrea felt her stomach roiling and she knew she had to find a bathroom fast before she embarrassed both of them.

“What's wrong?” he asked as she put a hand over her mouth.

“I think I am going to be sick Michael,” she gasped, pushing back the chair and hurrying to the ladies' room. Fortunately, she made it on time and threw up in the first bowl within reach. She was not aware that he had followed her and to her surprise he was there to hold her as she slid down on the floor.

He held her against him, not caring that she smelled of vomit and wiped the beads of sweat from her forehead. “You're going to have the restaurant thinking that we are going to sue them for food poisoning,” he teased her as he held her to him.

“We wouldn't want that,” she said weakly as she leaned back against his solid chest.

“Want to go home?” he asked her in concern.

“I am sorry Michael; I am just not feeling well.” She apologized. “I have gone ahead and spoiled our date.”

“We have many more dates so don’t worry about it.” He told her; helping her up and helping her rinse out her mouth.

He explained to the chef who came out personally to find out if everything was okay and insisted that they take home the food he had packaged for them.

He took her to his apartment and it was when she opened her eyes she realized that he had not taken her to her place. “I am spending more time here than at my place,” she told him with a small smile.

“I have already asked you to move in with me and you keep telling me no,” he said lightly; holding her hand as they stepped inside the elevator.

“I don’t have the strength to argue with you right now Michael,” she told him as he opened the door to let them into the building. He had been spending so many nights here that he had acquired a sofa where they could relax and watch television or play cards.

“I would never dream of arguing,” he told her airily, making sure she was comfortably ensconced in the plush sofa. “We need to talk,” he took a seat and put her feet on his lap.

Andrea looked at him askance. “Huh oh,” she murmured lightly.

He gazed at her in silence for a moment, his hand absently massaging her feet. “How do you feel about having children?”

“What?” she stared at him puzzled, this was certainly not what she expected to hear from him.

“Do you want children Andrea?” he asked her patiently.

“Eventually, yes,” she said impatiently.

“How about now?” he queried lightly, never taking his eyes from her.

“Now is certainly not a good time,” she told him firmly. “What are you getting at Michael?”

“When was the last time you had your period?” he probed.

“Don’t you think that’s a little personal, I-“ her eyes widened and she sat up as she realized what he was getting at. “You think I am pregnant?” she whispered.

He nodded; not daring to hope that she wanted a baby with him. Ever since she had run off to the bathroom he had been hoping the signs were pointing to that but he was worried she would not want a child. She had not told him she was even attracted to him; let alone that she loved him and he had too much pride to beg her.

Andrea sat there trying to think back to the last time she had had her monthly flow and realized with horror that it had been quite some time but she had been too busy to even notice. It all adds up. The dizzy spells, the nausea she felt when she the scent of certain food reached her and how her breasts felt tender.

She was aware that he was waiting for her to respond and knew he was anxiously awaiting her response but she had to process it first.

“I love you Andrea and I have asked you to marry me before. I am not asking again because I don’t want to crowd you with the way I feel. I would be honored if you were to consider having my baby but it's up to you and I will respect your decision in whatever you want." He told her quietly and Andrea felt humbled at how much he was baring his soul to her; this strong handsome man who could have had any woman he wanted; only wanted her and was willing to put up with whatever she threw at him.

"It's caught me by surprise, that's all," she told him. "And I don't want to get married because I might be pregnant Michael; this is not the dark ages."

"Why don't you want to marry me Andrea?" his hands were rigid against her legs and she knew it was getting to him, her supposed stubbornness about tying the knot. "Am I such a bad person that you won't give your total commitment to me?"

Andrea bit her lip as the feeling of fear shudder through her. The last thing on her mind had been marriage and having babies and now she was faced with both by the last person she had imagined being with. Michael Wade was rich and powerful and handsome and being his wife would require a lot from her; much more being the mother of his child and she did not know how it made her feel.

“I need time to think,” she told him slowly, deliberately ignoring the look of absolute disappointment on his face. She was certainly going to have the baby if she was pregnant; the baby had been conceived in passion and love but she needed time to sort things out in her mind.

“You got it,” he told her stonily. After moving her feet gently, he stood and went to the bathroom leaving her staring after him.

For the first time since they had been together; he did not sleep with her. She slept in the master bedroom and he spent the night in one of the smaller bedrooms. She found it hard to fall asleep and she kept hearing him pacing outside her door but he did not come in.

The next morning she went to her apartment and after making sure she was inside safe; he went away. They had not discussed anything and Andrea decided she was going to take a pregnancy test before they found out they were making a fuss over nothing.

The pregnancy test was positive and even though she was expecting it to be, Andrea stood there looking at the stick that had turned blue. She was going to have a baby. The thought hit her and she sat on the side of the bath; she had not taken this into consideration. A baby with Michael.

*****

He did not call her that night. She did not sleep well. She needed him beside her and especially now that she was scared and he was not here. The next morning at work he was not in the office and for a moment, she felt a sense of panic, wondering if he had ran off on her. But then common sense intervened and she shook off the unreasonable fear. Millie told her he had a meeting with some clients and wouldn't be in until late afternoon.

"Are you very busy?" Andrea asked the girl as she quickly took a seat beside her desk. There were not a lot of people in the office that knew about Michael and her dating but she had told Millie about Michael asking her to marry him.

"It depends on what you mean by busy," Millie teased as she put aside the documents she had been collating.

"I think I might be pregnant," she blurted out. Ever since she had found out, she had battled with sharing it with someone else apart from Michael who was upset with her at the moment.

Millie stared at her open mouthed for a moment. “Are you sure?” she looked at the slim beautiful girl with uncertainty. She had no idea the relationship had taken such a serious turn for Andrea.

“As sure as several pregnancy tests can be,” Andrea told her with a short laugh.

“Honey, Michael must be over the moon. I can just imagine what his mother has to say.” Millie said clapping her hands together in delight.

“Michael is upset with me because as he puts it: I stubbornly refuse to marry him and his mother does not know yet.” Andrea informed her.

“Why are you hesitating?” Millie demanded. “The man is in love with you; so please tell me what the problem is?”

“I can’t think about marriage right now Millie,” Andrea stood up agitated. “And Michael won’t see it my way, I asked him for some time to think and he is upset and it’s driving me crazy because he won't see reason. He is my employer and I can't separate him from being my lover; the two get mixed up."

"Andrea, you are my friend and I love you very much but you're a total idiot." Millie retorted. "It would just serve you right if he went and fell in love with someone else but smitten as he is; he will not be doing so. Put the man out of his misery and stop making him feel as if he is on a treadmill."

"Stop being so melodramatic," Andrea told her friend dryly; sitting back down. "I have a right to be careful."

"And you have a right to be happy and a man who loves you as well." Millie told her. "Don't let your past or what he does and used to do before, allow you to miss out on something wonderful. He is in love with you Andrea and you keep finding excuses why it should not be because of who he is, that's not fair to him."

Andrea was silent for a little while longer and then she admitted with a rueful smile. "I guess you're right."

"You know I am," Millie said firmly. "Now leave me alone and let me get some work done. How and when you are Mrs.

Hotshot Wade don't forget the little people who encouraged you."

"I am sorry who are you again?" Andrea grinned at the baleful glance her friend threw her; feeling lighter than she had felt in days. It was going to be fine, she thought, her hand unconsciously going to her flat stomach. She was having Michael's baby.

*****

Michael had finished the breakfast meeting an hour ago but still he lingered at the table in the restaurant. The meeting had gone well and he had a business deal to tie over in China in a few days. He was not sure he wanted to go anywhere with everything up in the air. He was thinking of sending one of the board members. Andrea was pregnant with his child and that was something he could not wrap his head around. He had always been so careful in the past because he would never dream of bringing a child casually into the world, no matter how much money he had. He had seen the ill effects of unwanted children and he had sworn he would never have a child with someone he was not totally in love with. And now that had happened and he was not sure the one he was in love with loved him back. The irony of it all. He thought wryly; the shoe is on the other foot.

Nonetheless, he was thrilled and he was sure he could convince Andrea that this was something wonderful. He had left her alone for the past two days and he had no intention of doing so now; she was carrying his child and as much as he wanted to put her over his shoulder and take her to the altar; he was going to respect her in that aspect but he was going to be there for her and his child whether she like it or not.

*****

She was waiting for him when he got back to his office and he deliberately dawdled at Millie's desk, collecting the messages and some documents she had for him to sign.

It was almost three thirty and he had planned to leave early to go and tell his mother the good news and of course call the family doctor to make an appointment to see him.

She closed the door behind him as soon as he was inside and with a brow rose, he turned towards her; waiting for her to say something.

"I am sorry," she told him; the words coming from her mouth as if she had been holding them in for a long time. Michael wanted to make it easy on her and pull her into his arms and tell her that he would go with whatever she decided but he decided to wait for her to speak.

"For what?" he asked her coolly.

"For making you think that I don't love you and I don't want you to think that I would not want to be your wife. I am cautious by nature Michael and past failed relationships have made me even more so. I am a little intimated by all this," she swept her hand around to encompass the building. "And I wonder if I will be able to cut it as your wife, so forgive me for being hesitant."

"Are you proposing to me?" he asked with a slightly crooked smile.

"Michael!" Andrea protested. "I am trying to say I love you and I don't want to lose you."

"You would have a hard time doing that Andrea," he told her huskily, coming around to pull her into his arms. "I am here to stay whether you like it or not." He murmured as he wrapped his arms around her and they came together for a passionate kiss.

*****

“I am going to be a grandmother!” Gloria screamed, hurrying forward to hug Andrea tightly to her, tears in her eyes. They left the office early to give his mother the good news and to make arrangements for the wedding. Andrea still trembled a little at the thought of marrying into such a powerful family but she knew it was going to be all right.

“Am I squeezing my grandchild?” she pulled back from Andrea and placed her hand over the girl’s flat stomach.

“There’s hardly any baby there to squeeze mom,” Michael said dryly, a foolish grin on his face. He felt like bursting with happiness and shouting it from the rooftops that Andrea had agreed to marry him and that she loved him and was carrying his child, everything else paled into insignificance.

“What’s this I hear about a small wedding?” Gloria said reproachfully, linking her arms with Andrea’s and leading her into the massive living room with its high ceiling and glittering chandelier. The first time she had been there she had been afraid to sit on the Regency made furniture. The place looked like a showpiece.

“Andrea does not want the entire country to attend our wedding and I think I agree with her.” Michael said as he joined them on the elegant white sofa. “The press is going to have a field day with the nuptials as it is without making it into a spectacle.”

“I am sorry Gloria but all this is quite overwhelming and Michael told me that as soon as they know I am pregnant they are going to hound me.” Andrea said a little unhappily.

Gloria laughed at the girl’s woebegone expression. “Darling, do like I do. Tell them to mind their own business and get on with your life. Yes, you’re going to be photographed and they are going to speculate and print all sorts of things but I have learned not to pay them any mind whatsoever.”

“So we will have a small intimate wedding with a few close friends and a press release after so that it does not look like we have something to hide.” Gloria said decisively. “But first we need to have Dr. Webb confirm your pregnancy, so I am going to give him a call to come over.”

“He makes house visits?” Andrea asked incredulously.

“He does for us,” Gloria said with an amused smile as she hurried from the room to call the doctor.

“How do you feel?” Michael asked her, pulling her closer to him.

“A little overwhelmed but otherwise okay I guess.” Andrea rested her head against his shoulder. She had started to feel a little dizzy but the feeling had settled down a bit. She had barely eaten some plain chicken soup for lunch and crackers to settle her stomach.

“You will get used to it,” Michael assured her softly. “I love you Andrea and the fact that you’re carrying my child makes me feel on top of the world. I can’t tell you how much I am in love with you right now.”

“I hope that feeling carries over to when I get big and fat and unsightly,” Andrea teased, her heart skipping a beat at his words. She never thought she would find love like this and she was hugging it close to her.

"You'll always be beautiful," Michael chided, lifting her chin and looking down at her; his green eyes bright with what he was feeling.

"Thanks," Andrea whispered as he bent his head and kissed her tenderly on the mouth.

"The doctor will be here shortly, so break it up you guys, we have a wedding to plan." Gloria bustled into the room; a pleased smile on her face. "I wished your father was here to see this," she said a suspicious sheen in her eyes as she came over and gave them a hug. "I am so happy I could just burst!"

Chapter 7

They were married in a private ceremony with a few friends and family to witness their nuptials. The press got wind of it and managed to snap a picture of them while they were coming out of the church. It was a lovely November morning with the fall leaves lying all around and the sun making a valiant effort to blaze through the clouds. The headline read: "Billionaire playboy and CEO of Wade Enterprises wed PRO Andrea Williams in private ceremony." It showed her going into the stretched limousine and laughing up at Michael as he helped her inside the vehicle.

Andrea realized she was getting a taste of what it was going to be like being married to Michael and she tried to squelch the feeling of panic that came over her. Her dress was of Venetian lace that looked more cream than white and been given to her by Gloria who had worn it all those years ago for her wedding. It was perfect on her; reaching a little past her knees and made entirely out of lace; it hugged her curvaceous body to perfection. Her breasts were fuller since her pregnancy and the bosom had to be let out somewhat.

They decided to forego the honeymoon for the time being because Andrea had been feeling well and she would not be able to do any length of traveling. Doctor Webb had done the examination and had said so far she was healthy and the best way to settle her stomach would be crackers and light meals every half an hour.

Andrea stared at the large diamond winking on her slim finger in wonder; she still could not believe she was married. She had given up her apartment and they were going to be staying in the family house; it had made his mother so happy and she had reorganized two suites for them complete with three bedrooms, a large kitchen, living room and two bathrooms. She was planning how to decorate the nursery. Michael was also keeping his apartment as well because as he put it, they might need some time away from all the luxury, he had told her with a grin.

They were at the apartment and she was recovering from a bout of nausea. He had taken a week from the office and they had decided to spend it at the apartment much to his mother's disappointment.

"How about some soup?" he asked in concern as she laid there on the bed; her stomach churning.

"No food," she told him shaking her head vehemently. He looked so lost and confused that Andrea felt sorry for him.

"What about a ginger ale?" he asked her sitting on the side of the bed and reaching for her hand. He still could not believe that this beautiful woman was his wife and even though she was going through a rough time with the pregnancy, he felt on top of the world.

"Are you going to be hovering over me the entire time?" she asked him teasingly.

"Absolutely," he told her with a gentle smile. "You're my wife so you're going to have to get used to pampering and spoiling."

"Is that so?" Andrea pulled him down beside her and went into his arms. He had wanted to take her on a Caribbean cruise but she had shied away from that knowing she would be sick the whole time. She had promised him that as soon as she felt better they would definitely be going. She was already two months pregnant and the doctor had told them after the first trimester her stomach would settle and she would be able to eat normal again.

They had discussed her role at the office and she had told him with determination that she was not going to stop working because she was very good at her job and she enjoyed it. She was not going to be some society wife and stayed home.

"But you're pregnant," he had protested.

"And what does that have to do with anything?" she had asked him; her hands on her hips.

"Why do I bother?" he had spread his hands in defeat. "I am never going to win an argument with you, am I?"

"No and get used to it," she had told him, reaching up to kiss him on the lips to soften the blow.

So now she was planning to go back to work when he did but she had told him that if she felt at all uncomfortable she would let him know and he would make sure she got some rest.

Millie had called to check up on her and told her to enjoy her honeymoon no matter how sick she felt because she was not going to get a lot of alone time when the baby came.

He made her some clear broth and to her surprise Andrea was able to hold it down. He had refused to take any calls from the office or do any work. He had canceled all his meetings until he got back. He was determined to wait on her hand and foot.

They were getting to know each other and Andrea loved the time they spent together. He had found a tiny restaurant that served delicious pasta and had driven out to buy her the pasta she loved.

"Will we be continuing the tradition of naming the baby Michael if it's a boy?" he asked her as they sat on the carpet in front of the fireplace; he was drinking wine and she a glass of milk because he had insisted on it.

"Why not?" Andrea said softly. The carpet was soft and thick and she dug her bare toes into it. She was snug and warm in a soft cotton robe. "Your dad is not alive so I think we should continue the tradition. What if it's a girl?"

"How about naming her after your mom?" he suggested.

Andrea stared at him wordlessly. They had spoke about her parents dying and how sad she still felt about them not being with her. "Annabelle?" she looked at him curiously; a smile on her face. "Isn't that too much for a little girl?"

"I think it's a lovely name," he told her firmly. "I can't think of a better name, can you?"

"Sometimes I wonder if I am going to wake up one morning and find out that you are just someone I dreamed up," Andrea said huskily, leaning back against him; his arms closing around her automatically.

"I went through life for a long time searching for something that I was not aware I was searching for and I have been around. I won't tell you otherwise and I never used a woman; we went into the relationship for mutual benefits and I did not mind giving financially because I was getting as much as I was giving." He paused and she looked up at him to see him staring down at her. "I always saw my mom and dad and the way they were into each other; I sometimes felt like the outsider, even though I knew they loved me but their love was so tangible that you could not help but notice it when they were with each other. I met you and I knew without a shadow of a doubt that I had found what I was looking for. With you, I have eyes for no one else. I love you Andrea Wade and that is something you are going to have to get used to."

Andrea felt the tears starting and she knew it was partly because of the raging hormones going through her body; a body that was forming a baby they had made but it was mostly because of what he said. "I love you my darling, magnificent husband," she told him; her throat aching with unshed tears as he bent his head and took her lips with his in a passionate kiss that weakened her before lifting her up and taking her to their bedroom.

*****

He took her shopping for winter clothes and even though she was still not showing they shopped for maternity clothes and went to baby stores to peek at the little clothes that seemed too tiny to cover a real person.

A photographer caught them coming out of the baby store and hurriedly snapped their picture, a candid shot that showed Michael gazing down at her tenderly as she smiled up at him. It came out the very next day with the headline: "Shopping for Baby?" With the questions asked if the Wade's were expecting an addition to the family and if that was the real reason for the private ceremony. Michael was anxious that it would upset her but Andrea told him she did not mind one bit.

He did not allow her to do anything and she was getting frustrated with the inactivity so they went to visit his mother as they would be going there in a couple of days. The suite of rooms had been transformed and Gloria happily showed them the beginning of the nursery.

“It’s beautiful Gloria but you don’t have to go through so much trouble.” Andrea protested giving her mother in law a fond hug.

“Nonsense darling. I love doing it, decorating is in my bones.” Gloria linked her hand through hers and they went off without Michael to walk around the large airy room that had different paraphernalia that screamed baby. Andrea could not get over how impressive and huge the house was and their suite of rooms had been done over in soft pastel colors that Andrea found relaxing.

It was almost Thanksgiving and Gloria was planning a huge party to show her off as she put it. Andrea was not sure she was up to it but she did not want to disappoint this wonderful woman who had taken her into the fold without hesitation.

They had dinner and discussed the living arrangements.

“I promise I won’t hover excessively and be in your way,” Gloria told them seriously as she dabbed her lips delicately with the napkin. Andrea smiled her thanks at Bertie as the woman removed her plate. She had managed to eat beef stew without her stomach being upset and she had noticed Michael looking at her anxiously while she ate. She had smiled at him reassuringly and nodded.

“I am sure you won’t get in our way Mom; this house is big enough to hold a football team.” Michael told his mother dryly.

Gloria flashed him a fond smile. “So both of you are going back to the office on Monday? Are you sure it’s not too soon dear?” she turned to look at Andrea.

“I need to work Gloria and please don’t encourage Michael, he thinks I should be staying home and resting as if I am going through some sort of illness.” Andrea said wryly, giving her husband a teasing glance.

“I just told her to take another week and you would be here with her if anything happens,” Michael said with a shrug. “Not that anything is going to happen,” he hastened to say, reaching for her hand on the table. “I wish you would reconsider baby,”

“I will be fine,” Andrea said with a gentle smile. “You’re going to be there hovering over me; it’s a wonder if I will get anything done. And besides we have the grand opening of the hotel and the pharmacy to deal with and I have some press releases to send out.”

“You see what I have to deal with Mom?” Michael sighed dramatically, tightening his hold on her hand and as Gloria watched her son and daughter in law; she was reminded of how it was with she and her husband. They had been so in love that she had not noticed any one around when they were together. She felt a sharp stab of pain, missing him was too intense she felt like crying. She had been able to put the whole devastating loss aside because of what was happening with her son and his wife but seeing them together brought back so much pain.

“Mom, you okay?” Michael asked her; staring at her in concern.

“Just feeling a little de trop that’s all,” she told him lightly. No need to put a pall over their happiness.

“Honey can you get me some tea please?” Andrea asked her husband; looking at her mother in law shrewdly. “You know the one you make for me to settle my stomach?”

He stood up hastily and went towards the kitchen.

“His father used to spoil me rotten too,” Gloria said with a smile as she watched her son strode out of the dining room.

“You miss him a lot don’t you?” Andrea said sympathetically, reaching for the woman’s hand.

“Desperately,” Gloria admitted with a shaky laugh. “I am sorry to put a pall on your happiness dear.”

“Nonsense,” Andrea said gently. “I just want you to know that I am here for you whenever you need a shoulder to cry on. I know I am not your daughter by birth but I would like to think I am your daughter nonetheless.”

“You are my daughter,” the woman said firmly, giving the girl’s hand a squeeze. “I am so happy you two found something that is so rare. I have loved and have been loved by a wonderful man and for that I am very thankful. Michael Senior made me feel special every time we were together, that never changed.

We had a few arguments," she laughed suddenly, her face softened with the memories of the past. "But we managed to sort them out before we went to bed and the making up of it was always beautiful."

"Michael makes me feel that way too," Andrea said with a whimsical smile. "He treats me like Dresden china and sometimes I get a little impatient with him hovering all the time, but I must admit that I love it and I love him so much I can't believe it sometimes."

"Treasure it my dear," Gloria told her. "It's one of the most precious thing in the world; this love that we experience. A lot of people get married because it's expected of them and they spend their lives being so miserable together. I have friends who have been divorced up to four times and collecting alimony checks is what their lives are all about. Filling the empty space up with shopping. I had Michael and I had a wonderful marriage that will take me throughout life and a son from that marriage that was mad in love."

Andrea smiled at the woman and realized she had something so rare and special that she should spend her life appreciating it and never taking it for granted.

Michael came back just then with the steaming cup of tea and Andrea realized then that he could have asked Bertie to make it and take it to her but he had done so himself. She pulled down his head towards hers as he put the tea in front of her and kissed him softly on the lips. “I love you very much.” She whispered.

“I love you too, baby.” He told her. If he was surprised at the sheen of tears in her eyes, he did not mention it.

Gloria looked at them with satisfaction, no longer feeling sad as she gave a contented sigh.

*****

They spent the night there, much to Gloria’s delight. They spent some time talking with Gloria telling her about some of Michael’s exploits as a child which had Andrea laughing merrily. She was not aware that her husband was taking in her every laughter and body movements; a look of intense love on his face.

That night in bed he told her about the relationship he had had with his dad and how special it had been.

"He never told me that I had to go and get a business degree in order to take over the business from him," Michael said reflectively, stroking her arm as she rested her head on his shoulder. His mother had retired to her suite of rooms with a smile on her face and that was what Andrea had hoped to see; that's the reason she had gently but casually suggested to Michael that they spend the night. "He was always telling me to follow my dreams and whatever I wanted to do he would support me."

"He was a very good father," Andrea commented softly, her eyes closing in contentment as she snuggled closer to him; this man who was her husband.

"The best," Michael agreed, wrapping his hands around her. "We did a lot of things together and even though he hated my lifestyle, he never condemned me; maybe because as mom said, before he met her he was a lot like me." He grinned.

"You miss him don't you?" she lifted her head to stare down at him.

"Too much," he admitted with a sad smile. "And this house reminds me so much of him; sometimes it hurts to come here."

“Can you just imagine how your Mom feels?” she asked him softly, reaching up a hand to stroke his strong hair roughened cheek. He needs a shave, she thought absently. “She misses him so much Michael and it cannot be easy for her to be here alone in this huge place with only her memories to console her; that’s why I said we should stay the night.”

“I know and I know how much she appreciates that,” he raised his head up to kiss her lips. “She is going to spoil our baby terribly; I hope you’re prepared for that.”

“I am,” Andrea nodded; her lips tingling from his kiss.

“Dad told me when he met mom there was no other woman for him,” Michael told her. “And now I am telling you the same Andrea; it’s you and only you.”

“I know,” Andrea whispered softly, resting her head on his chest. He was the only man for her as well.

*****

On the other side of the house in her suite Gloria flipped through the beautiful gold embossed baby album filled with the different stages of Michael from babyhood to about seven years old. Her fingers lingered lovingly over one with him dressed in a pale blue suit when he was about two months old. She remembered the day as if it was yesterday. She and Michael had been taking him to church to be blessed and she remembered how fearful she had been because as she told her husband; the water might be too cold. He had laughingly told her that she was turning into a neurotic mother.

She had been so possessive that even though she loved her husband; had found it hard to let him hold their son. It had taken a while for her to let go of that and her husband, instead of being upset, had allowed her to grow out of that feeling all by herself.

She had seen the looks exchanged between her son and his wife and it had brought her back to her own relationship with her husband. There had been times when they did not have to say a word to each other but with just a touch or a look they would know what the other was thinking or needed. He was the love of her life and there was no finding that no matter where she went.

She closed the album and hugged it to her, a smile on her face. Her husband was gone physically but there were additions to the family; she had gotten a daughter and now there was going to be a grandchild as well.

Chapter 8

They went into work together Monday morning and were greeted with cheers as they made their way to their offices. To her surprise, she was greeted respectfully as Mrs. Wade during the course of the day and sometimes it took a while for her to realize that they were addressing her. People in the company who had, in the past just barely waved to her were now at her beck and call and as she told Millie; she was not used to this kind of attention.

“Get used to it,” Millie said with a wicked smile; giving her friend a quick hug as Andrea sat at the chair beside her desk. The girl had been beautiful before but now she had a kind of ethereal beauty that had Millie staring at her. “Mrs. Wade how are you?”

“Don’t you start,” Andrea said with a laugh. She had been there since eight that morning and had protested because Michael had wanted them to come in later. He had spent the better part of the morning checking up on her until in exasperation she had told him if he came into her office one more time she was going to lock the door on him.

"That's what I get for being a concerned husband," he had grumbled to Millie as he went back into his office. "Make sure she doesn't over tax herself." He had said as he strode back into his office.

"I am doing well thank you," she answered Millie's question; gesturing impatiently for the receptionist to come in as the girl stopped just outside the doorway as soon as she saw her. "The queasiness is kind of abating and for that I am very happy." The girl gave her a nervous smile as she handed Millie a package that had just arrived before hurrying out of the office. "They do know that I am the same person don't they?" she asked Millie wryly.

"Same person who now bears the name Wade and is carrying the heir to the fortune," Millie told her airily. "You can't be expected to be treated the same way honey. Heck I am your friend and sometimes I have to wonder if I am being too facetious in calling you Andrea."

"I am still Andrea and if you dare call me otherwise I will not be responsible to what I use to hit you with," Andrea warned her friend as she stood up to leave.

"Okay Mrs. Wade," Millie called after her.

Andrea sent her a killing glance before going into her office.

*****

She spent the rest of the day tying up loose ends for the opening of the two companies and every now and then Michael sent the chef with something for her to eat; not daring to face her himself. Andrea smiled as she saw that he was standing just outside her office looking at her, making sure she was eating.

“Aren’t you coming in?” she asked him archly; pushing away the bowl of broth she had been eating.

“I was told I would be locked out if I ventured in,” he said in an offensive tone.

“You may come in,” she nodded her head regally; an impish smile on her face.

“You have me wrapped around your little finger; I hope you know that,” he said with a sigh as he kissed her passionately on the mouth.

“Likewise,” she said huskily, holding on to him and returning the kiss.

“How are you feeling?” he pressed a hand to her still flat stomach.

“A little queasy but we are okay.” She told him.

“Good,” he sat on the chair beside the desk. She still had not gone back to her old office even though it had been repainted and refurnished; she had told Michael that she still had visions of David Baker there whenever she passed by the room. His wife and children had been generously taken care of by the company; all Michael’s idea and for that Andrea was glad. “Now tell me about the ideas you have for the opening of the two companies.”

Andrea showed him what she had come up with and they spent the next hour making several changes and discussing what to send out in the press release.

They left the office at six and for that Michael was adamant; insisting that she had done enough for the day and it was time to go home or else she would not be coming in the morning.

“I don’t answer to you anymore as your employee Michael,” she told him frostily as he picked up the files on her desk and dumped them into the desk drawer. “I am your wife.”

"That's correct and right now I am using the husband card," he told her firmly, taking up her pocketbook.

She was upset with him until they got inside the car where he opened the glove compartment and took out a jewelry box. Inside was an exquisitely made slender chain with a topaz stone winking in the dim light. She stared at it wordlessly as he reached inside the box and pulled out the chain and put it around her neck. "Just a little something to say I love you," he told her softly as he positioned the stone properly between her cleavage. "And because it brings out the gold color in your eyes.

Andrea flung her hands around his neck and with tears in her eyes she whispered. "I love you my husband."

"I love you too Mrs. Wade." He held her to him gently. They stayed that way for a little bit before he drove them home.

*****

The opening for the pharmaceutical company was a huge hit. Andrea had come up with the idea of killing two birds with one stone and having the opening in the newly renovated 'Wade luxury hotel' and the designers had worked feverishly to get both buildings ready. There was a huge crowd and the press was there in their numbers, Andrea had seen to that. After the pall that had been put on the company by the suicide of David Baker, she had made sure they put a positive spin on it. She had hired the very best caterers and had been with them in the planning of the menu much to Michael's protestations of her working too hard. "Let me do my job darling," she had told him with a quick kiss before hurrying out to see to something else. His mother who had been there in the office for a board meeting had told him with a laugh, "Let her be honey, she will know when to slow down."

She had started showing a little bit and had chosen to wear a stunning dark blue gown that shimmered every time she moved. Michael had taken her shopping and had practically bought out the store. Diamonds blazed at her throat, ears and wrists and she and her husband made a stunning couple as they moved among the crowd with the ease of people who had been doing it for a long time.

Gloria waved at them from across the room where she was being entertained by a group of business men who had been friends with her husband. She was wearing pale green silk that looked lovely on her. Ever since they had officially moved into the house, she had been a happier person. She and Andrea were decorating the nursery together even though they did not yet know the sex of the baby.

The caterers made sure she was supplied with orange juice the whole evening and to her delight she found she could eat the delicacies provided without rushing to the ladies' room. The hotel was booked to capacity for the winter season and Andrea had come up with the idea of having a play area in one of the rooms for children to hang out.

"Tired?" Michael murmured into her ear. He had to admit that she had done an exceptional job and as much as he would prefer that she slow things down; he had to give her credit where credit was due.

"No," she whispered back. "I am having a very good time."

"You do know you are the most beautiful woman in the room don't you?" he asked her.

"I expect you to say that, you're my husband." Andrea teased.

“Not true, I did a survey and all the men agree with me,” he told her solemnly. “My wife is the most beautiful woman they have ever seen.”

“You’re going to have to show me that survey,” she laughed up at him. That’s how the camera captured them and the photo that was splashed across the papers the next day; along with a detailed description of the luxury of the hotel and how good the food was. It also mentioned the who's who of society that had been present and predicted that the hotel was going to a raging success. It also mentioned that the pharmaceutical company was up and running under new management and that they expect great things. The article had a spread about Michael Wade, the son who took over the running of the company after his father’s tragic accident and was doing a very good job.

There was a general air of celebration at work that week and a lot of congratulations to Andrea for the job she was doing. “We’re going to miss you when you go off Mrs. Wade,” a board member said with a genuine smile as he came from Michael’s office while she was on her way in.

“What does he mean by that?” she asked her husband. It had been a week since the opening and she was working on a high end department store they had acquired.

Michael looked up at her with a smile. She was starting to show and she looked lovely and elegant in her maternity wear. “What?”

“Clyde Manning just said ‘We are going to miss you when you go off’, what does he mean by that?” she asked him.

“He probably means when you go off for several months or a year for your maternity leave,” Michael told her patiently.

“No one goes off on maternity leave for a year or six months Michael so what are you talking about?” she asked him with a frown.

“You are not just anyone Andrea,” he told her with a sigh, knowing he was in for a big argument. “You’re the wife of the CEO and you’re carrying my baby so you are different.”

“I am not going off for a year Michael,” she told him decidedly. “Nor for several months; while you are here working, it’s not fair.”

“Can we discuss this when we get home honey?” he asked her pleadingly. “I am asking nicely and I bet when the baby comes along you are going to want to stay home.”

“Not a chance,” she warned him; turning to leave.

“Baby, there is something I want to discuss with you and I want you to be reasonable.” Michael said before she could leave.

“I am always reasonable,” she told him turning around.

“Diana has been calling me and crying, saying I left her and now I am married. She wants to see me.” He looked at her cautiously. He had debated whether or not to tell her but had decided he would never keep secrets from her, no matter how unpleasant.

“When did she call?” Andrea asked him calmly.

“She called again a few minutes ago. Andrea, you know I would not encourage her; I love you and I would never do anything to hurt you.” Michael came around from his desk and stood in front of her

"I know," she told him softly, placing a hand on his cheek. He closed his eyes in relief and placed his hand on hers. "If I lost you to someone else I would probably behave the same way too. I will talk to her."

"What?" his eyes snapped open in surprise.

"I need her number to call her, I will talk to her." Andrea repeated.

"Andrea you can't," he protested. Damn! He thought in despair, what was he going to do? "I don't want her saying something to hurt your feelings."

"I promise you I will be polite and understanding and tell her exactly why she cannot call my husband anymore." Andrea explained to him.

Michael still looked undecided but he reluctantly gave her the number; his heart heavy.

"Don't worry darling, it's going to be okay, you'll see." Andrea gently kissed him on the cheek before heading out.

*****

She invited the girl out to lunch at the new hotel restaurant and she was greeted by the manager himself who made sure she had a very good table. She had told Michael about the lunch date and he had told her he did not think it was a good idea. She should call and cancel or maybe he should call and cancel. She had reminded him that he was not going to be doing any calling to that number again.

The girl walked into the restaurant and heads turned. Andrea smiled wryly as she remembered how much she had been intimidated by the girl's physical beauty not too long ago. She was wearing a black silk sheath that wrapped her slender body like a glove and her raven black hair was piled carelessly on top of her head as if she was going for casual chic but did not quite succeed. She was truly a beautiful woman.

She summoned the waiter before she reached the table and ordered a glass of champagne, in the middle of the day, this girl was high maintenance; Andrea thought with a small smile.

"Hi Diana, nice to finally meet you, I am a fan of yours." Andrea said graciously, extending a hand. The girl hesitated before taking it and then sat down gracefully.

“Thanks,” her voice was sultry. “I don’t know what you hope to accomplish with this lunch Mrs. Ah – Andrea,” she said quickly and with quick insight she realized she was avoiding calling her by her married name as if that could change the fact that she was married to Michael.

“I just want to sort out some things between us,” she told the girl pleasantly, smiling as the waiter brought her orange and fruit punch juice and champagne for Diana. “Thanks Donald.”

“What things?” Diana sipped champagne with appreciation at the texture and the body, she had gotten used to the good things in life and she found she could not do without them. That was why it made her so mad that this little nobody had snagged the most eligible man he had ever met.

“You are an extraordinarily beautiful woman,” Andrea began. “You don’t need to be calling my husband and begging him to talk to you. You are worth more than that. He’s in love with me and I am sorry if you were hurt when the relationship did not work out but you need to move on; for someone as beautiful as you are, you can have just about any man you want.”

“I can and I can also have Michael if I wanted him back,” she said spitefully expecting the girl to get angry. How dare she lecture her on relationships? Who did she think she was? "Did he tell you how much fun we had in bed? How he could not get enough of me?" she asked cattily. They had been served the chef's special, a salad that tasted like this side of heaven.

"That's where you are wrong my dear girl," Andrea told her smoothly helping herself to the delicious salad. "You cannot have him back because he is with me now and no matter how much fun you had in bed that's neither here nor there. I consider it in total bad taste to discuss what a person does in bed. And I am telling you nicely right now that I don't want you calling my husband again."

"And if I still do?" Diana asked outraged.

"Then I would have to call the agent representing you and have a little talk with her. It's Barlow's Agency isn't it?" she went on without waiting for a response. "I believe Wade Enterprises has shares in it am I wrong?"

"You wouldn't dare!" the girl hissed, pushing away her plate of salad.

"Try me," Andrea said with a deathly expression on her face. "Move on and I will stay out of your way; don't and I promise you I will be the end of your very promising career. We are a family now; it's not just Michael and I but there is going to be a baby involved and I will not stand by and allow you to destroy what we have."

There was silence for a few seconds as the girl digested what she just said and then without a word she stood in graceful fluid movement. "I was getting a little bored with him in the end anyway," she said sulkily.

"Good, so I guess we won't be hearing from you again?" Andrea asked her politely. "Very nice to meet you though, still a very big fan."

The girl left without saying another word and Andrea sat there laughing silently finishing her lunch. That was that.

*****

Michael paced the office constantly looking at the clock on his desk. Every few minutes he asked Millie if she had heard from his wife and when Millie answered no he had been tempted to call her himself. What was he thinking? Letting her go to the damn lunch with Diana. But then again when has she ever listened to him? He thought in despair. Never.

He was about to call her himself when she walked into the office. It was after two o'clock and she had been gone for the past hour and a half.

"So how did it go?" he asked trying to be casual.

"Were you worried about something?" she asked him sweetly as she came towards him. "Because Millie told me that you have been asking every five minutes if she's heard from me. What were you worried about my husband?" she looped her hands around his neck and his body sagged in relief. That meant it went well.

"I wasn't worried," he told her blithely, kissing her cold cheeks. "How did it go?"

"Very well. I just told her why it would not be a good idea for her to call you again and she agreed." Andrea told him.

"Just like that?" he asked her suspiciously.

"Just like that." She told him with a smile.

"Okay," he said uncertainly and bent to kiss her lips before letting her go.

“And darling,” she stopped at the door. “Lose her number.”

“Already did,” he told her solemnly; gazing after her in wonder.

*****

They were having dinner later that day when Michael told Gloria about it. “I thought I was going to have a heart attack when she told me she was having lunch with Diana. I kept pacing the office and getting Millie annoyed with me because I was asking her every second if my wife had called.” He said ruefully. “You’re going to be the death of me one day.”

“I most certainly am not,” Andrea told him loftily, spooning the soup into her mouth.

Gloria laughed so hard that she had to put away her spoon. “I remember a similar incident with your father. This woman kept calling his phone and he was too polite to ask her to stop calling so I had to do it for him. I am interested to know what you told her dear,” she looked at her daughter in law in admiration. “That girl is known to be very pushy and rude; what did you say to her?”

“I just told her that if she continued calling my husband I would have to have a talk with her agency about her practice of harassing my family. I am now a pregnant wife and you know what the stress can do.” Andrea said with a grin.

“You didn’t!” Gloria gasped.

“You did not tell me that Andrea,” Michael looked at her with a slight frown.

“You did not need to know,” Andrea arched a brow at him. “She was getting pushy and telling me how much fun you two had in bed so had to say something to make her know that I am not afraid of what she had to say.”

“She said that to you?” Michael was furious. “That’s why I did not want you to have lunch with her Andrea. She is not the nicest person and she will say things to deliberately hurt you.”

“It sounds to me that your wife handled herself just fine Michael,” his mother said mildly.

“You underestimate me darling,” Andrea chided. “Just out of curiosity; are there any more I need to be preparing for?”

“No,” he told her softly, his expression apologetic. “I am sorry baby; I just did not want you to have to go through that.”

“That’s okay,” Andrea leaned over and kissed him on the cheek. “I don’t have a problem with your past as long as it’s your past. Just know that if it happens in the present or the future then you’re going to have to deal with me and I fight mean.”

Gloria laughed in delight at the expression on her son’s face and looked as her daughter in law continue to eat her meal as if she had just something casual. The girl was someone to contend with. Good for her.

Chapter 9

It was almost Christmas and with it icy cold without even a drop of snow. Andrea had gotten bigger and she complained to her husband that she looked like a truck.

"You look like a beautiful truck," he teased her as he came up behind her as she was putting on her makeup.

"You were supposed to say: 'Of course not'," Andrea said dryly leaning back against him as he put his hands on her belly possessively. He had taken to talking to the baby every chance he got and she had complained that he was totally ignoring the person carrying the baby.

"Oh forgive me for being honest," he bent his head to nibble her ear. She was five months pregnant and the ultra sound had said it was going to be a boy. "Lord help us another Michael!" Andrea had teased.

"Are you sure you're up to coming into the office?" he asked her in concern. She had been feeling down for the past few days and had to come home a little early to get some rest.

"Yes I am," she told him firmly. "The people at work are worse than your mother; I am being coddled to death. It's bad enough you have told everyone to report to you if I'm doing too much. Now you have everyone watching my every move, I can't pee without somebody asking me if I am okay." She said in an annoyed tone.

"Can you blame me for being so concerned?" he protested, moving away from her a little bit because he had discovered that his wife was not a woman to put up with nonsense. "You refuse to take it easy, no matter what I or the doctor say to you so you leave me no choice. Damn Andrea, bad enough you don't listen to me at home but my staff are going to think I have no control over my wife so how am I going to run a company?"

"Your staff are not foolish enough to think your wife needs controlling and your track record in running the company speaks for itself." She retorted as she finished applying her make-up. "Okay fine, I will try to play the submissive wife when we are at work, how about that?"

Michael shook his head and pulled her into his arms; an indulgent smile on his face. "You couldn't be submissive if you tried." He kissed her on the lips passionately, totally ruining the lip gloss she had just applied but that did not matter to his wife one bit.

*****

The staff party was held at the office and with the exchange of gifts. The office was going to be closed for two weeks. Michael was planning for them to go up to the log cabin that belonged to the family for a week. His mother was going away on a cruise with friends because she could not bear to stay at the home where she had always spent Christmas with her husband. Andrea and Michael had urged her to come with them but she had told them they did not need an old woman tagging after them and being in their way.

It was a half day at the office and the day before Christmas Eve. Andrea had gone out with Millie to do a little last minute shopping. Michael had given her so much; buying her gifts for no apparent reason and plying her with jewelry and clothes and had even bought her a brand new Corvette, even though she still continued to drive to work with him.

"When am I going to get the chance to drive it?" she had protested; her hands going to her throat as she stared at the shiny new vehicle when he had brought her down to the massive garage to show her. Gloria had been there and admired the vehicle. There were already four cars in the garage and hers would make five. “There are three of us living here and five cars; when are we going to drive the rest?”

“A thank you will do,” her husband had said dryly, handing her the keys.

“Thanks, my husband,” she wrapped herself in his arms and planted a big kiss on his lips. “I could get used to all this spoiling.”

“You’re supposed to be,” he grinned at her as he held her close to him.

“His father did the same for me,” Gloria said softly, looking at the couple mistily.

“Are you okay?” Andrea let go of Michael and went over to give her mother in law a hug.

“I am dear,” she told the girl with a fond smile. She was very happy they were there with the holidays coming up. The most painful part of losing her husband was the holidays, it was not so bad because they were there.

They had taken the car for a test drive around the block and Andrea thought it handled like a dream; so unlike her old car that was always giving her trouble.

"What on earth do you buy for a family that has everything?" Andrea said in exasperation. They had been walking around the crowded mall for the past hour and she had seen nothing she liked.

"You do realize that you can simply place an order from one of the many stores that Wade Enterprises have accounts with don't you?" Millie asked her. She had already bought some things for her family and was now helping Andrea look for her gifts.

"I know but then it would not have the personal touch," Andrea said. The mall was alive with beautiful decorations Santa everywhere and the Christmas carols came over the hidden speakers. The spirit of Christmas was in the air.

"How about a sweater?" Millie suggested, gesturing towards a clothing section.

“He has a million sweaters and a million of everything else,” Andrea said in despair. “The man has more clothes than a clothing store.”

Millie laughed. “How about a watch?” and seeing the expression on her friend’s face she said hastily. “I know he has a million of those as well but what about one that is engraved: ‘To my darling husband Michael with love your wife Andrea’”

Andrea’s eyes lit up. “That’s a great idea but will it be ready for tomorrow?” she worried.

“Honey the name Wade carries a lot of weight so just start throwing it around.” Millie reminded her.

Andrea did, albeit reluctantly as the jeweler told her that with the Christmas rush upon them it was too last minute. As soon as she mentioned who she was, she was told that it would be ready in the next fifteen minutes if it’s not too much trouble.

“I told you,” Millie told her with a smile. “If you have it why not flaunt it?”

"You're a bad influence," Andrea told her dryly as they went to get a silk scarf for Gloria. She bought a beautiful cashmere sweater and a matching scarf for Millie; an Ipad for her daughter Simone and a beautiful hand tooled leather briefcase for Mark.
"This is way too much," Millie protested as Andrea had them gift wrapped individually and handed the packages to her friend. She had given Andrea a beautiful scarf for her gift.

"I have the money and Michael told me to use my credit cards," Andrea told her dryly. "I am spending on my friends so allow me to do so."

"Thanks," Millie said huskily, giving her friend a hug. "It pays to have a friend who has money," she teased.

Instead of having the usual large party that people had become accustomed to over the years, they had decided to have an intimate dinner at home and had invited Millie and her family as well as a few of Michael's friends and Gloria's as well.

They walked around the mall for a little bit, killing time until the watch was ready and they went into a baby store to exclaim over the tiny clothes there. She and Millie ended up buying a few things that they could not resist.

*****

They got back to the office a few minutes after two. Michael was in a meeting with the board tying up loose ends before the holiday break. The hotel was doing very well and the pharmaceutical company was slowly getting back on its feet with an entirely new management team. Andrea made sure she had finished working with whatever she had on her desk. Michael had gone over her head and hired an assistant for her; to take some of the work load from her; he had said, avoiding her eyes.

The girl was a very young twenty and very eager to please. She got on her nerves most of the time until she was tempted to tell Michael she was going to send her to his office but she was working out finally because Andrea had told her to forget that she was married to the CEO of the company and just get the job done.

He came out of the meeting looking a bit tired but his face lit up as soon as he came by her office and saw that she was there. “Hey, I didn’t know you were back,” he came around to her desk to pluck her from her chair and kissed her much to the acute embarrassment of Claudia, her assistant who mumbled a hurried good afternoon and scuttled out.

“Now see what you did, frightened the poor girl away.” Andrea reproached him with a smile.

“That girl is like a frightened rabbit,” he said shaking his head as he placed his hands on her extended belly.

“Why do you look so tired?” she asked him concerned as she used her hands to frame his face; her eyes searching every inch of his face.

“I am a little drained,” he admitted. He did not dare hide anything from her because she did not let go until he told her what was up. “I am thinking if it’s a good idea to buy into the company we had discussed before. It seems to be more trouble than it’s worth.”

“So put off on buying it until you have all the details and it can always wait until we get back.” Andrea advised. She loved that he always discussed business with her. She had told him she was not the kind of wife that wanted to look pretty and not bother her head about things like the business aspect. She wanted to hear everything and she was not going to faint away if things got too harsh.

“The board is eager to get on with it because they said a rival company is fishing around and it’s on a prime location.” Michael said.

“Do your homework honey and don’t let the board pressure you into doing something that you will regret.” Andrea said firmly.

“Yes ma'am,” he kissed her lingeringly on the lips and then his eyes caught the packages in the corner. “You think you did enough shopping?” he asked raising a brow.

“Maybe not,” she told him with a straight face. They had a mountain of gifts underneath the towering Christmas tree that all three of them had decorated. “I finally get to use the cards you gave me because you keep buying me things,” she pouted.

“You don’t complain because you hate to shop,” he reminded her. “You’re unlike any woman I have ever known.”

“You’d do well to remember that,” she told him, placing a tender hand against his cheek. “I love you Michael Wade.”

“I love you so much Andrea Wade,” he told her softly, hugging her to him. She broke the contact and told him she had work to finish up.

“We’re not leaving late today,” he warned her as he went back to his office.

She nodded, her attention already on the document she had on her desk.

*****

For someone who had spent most Christmas's by herself apart from last year when she had had dinner with Millie; this time it was extra special and she felt like a kid waiting up for Santa to make his appearance. She shook Michael awake that morning and he had jumped up thinking that something was wrong with her or the baby.

“It’s time to open the presents,” she told him excitedly.

“So you’re okay?” he asked her; staring at her.

“Of course I am,” she told him impatiently, pushing the comforter off them and getting ready to climb off the huge four poster bed.

“Andrea it’s four a.m. on a holiday,” Michael protested; glancing at the red lights of the bedside clock. He smiled indulgently at the animated expression on her beautiful face and caught on to her excitement. He had taken these things for granted over the years because he had gotten used to getting expensive gifts from his parents but he realized that all this was new to her and that’s was what made spoiling her so much fun. She was not like the jaded women he was used to; who took the gifts he gave them without so much as a thank you.

She dragged him downstairs where the beautiful Christmas tree blinked its dozens of lights that played on the gaily wrapped gifts under the tree.

His mother was already there, wrapped up in her old flannel robe, a big smile on her face. She had been the only one enthused over Christmas over the years and now she had gotten company.

His child like wife sat on the carpeted floor and started handing out gift wrapped packages to them and began tearing into her piles of gifts which was much bigger than that of her husband and mother in law.

Her husband joined her on the floor and he and his mother watched as she opened each gift and screamed in delight. She had gotten several article of clothing, like she needed more. Sweaters ranging from different colors and she got a beautiful diamond bracelet from Gloria and matching earrings. The last package she opened had a smaller box inside and when Andrea opened it she was speechless. It was a blazing sapphire necklace suspended on a thin platinum chain and the stone sparkled in the dim light. It was incredibly beautiful and she could not stop staring at it. “It’s safe to say that this is by far the best Christmas I have ever had.” She said huskily, holding on to her husband’s hand. He helped her up and she went into his arms; tears in her eyes. “Thanks” she whispered, moving to include her mother in law in the embrace.

They had eggnog and Andrea was allowed to drink a little bit because of the alcohol content. She sat snuggled in her husband’s arms as they sat in the living room in front of the blazing fire.

They had breakfast prepared by Gloria. Ham and eggs and toast with milk and orange juice for Andrea as she was banned from drinking coffee during her pregnancy. They spent the rest of the morning preparing for the dinner later that evening. Gloria had given the staff the time off but Bertie had prepared the bulk of the food such as the turkey, roast beef and chicken and the baked macaroni and cheese so Andrea helped Gloria do up the salads. Bertie had also made sweet potato pies and pumpkin pies which would be served with whipped cream and ice cream.

*****

The dinner was a success and there was general air of celebration and happiness. Simone hugged her and told her that she loved her gift. The meal was consumed rapidly and Gloria watched as her son kept making sure that his wife was okay and she was not getting sick. Andrea's face was animated as she laughed at something Millie's husband said to her. The girl's happiness made her feel lighter than she had felt in several months and she knew that having her around had done a lot for her and Michael.

"I want to make a toast," she stood up suddenly. She looked beautiful in a red sweater and a black wool pants; her blonde hair swept on top of her head. "We experienced a great tragedy when my husband's plane went down several months ago. Michael and I thought there was no way we would ever be happy again. We were wrong," she smiled, her eyes turning to her daughter in law. "Andrea came into our lives and she is unlike any person we have ever met. She has managed to tame my son, so you can just imagine what I am talking about." Those at the table laughed along with her and her son threw her a wry look. "She has brought back Christmas to this household and I want to personally tell her that she is by far the best person I know. I love her, not like a daughter in law, but like a daughter. I am asking you to lift your glasses with me and cheer this lovely young woman that is like a diamond among us."

Everyone called out cheers and Andrea felt her throat clog up and she could not speak. They had given her more than she had ever dreamed of and Gloria was saying that she had given more.

She stood up and with tears in her eyes she said: "I have married into the most wonderful family in the world and I am so thankful. Sometimes I wonder if this is something real or will I wake up and see that I had been sleeping. My husband told me it's real and I am not dreaming so I guess I have to believe him." She smiled tremulously as she turned to him. "I love you Michael Wade and I will not get tired of saying it. Gloria your are a mother to me and I love you so much; I am so spoiled that sometimes I don't know how to deal with it. Thanks very much." She went over and kissed her mother in law and then went to stand beside her husband as he closed his arms around her.

It was a beautiful Christmas and one she would never forget no matter what.

*****

The time spent at the cabin was relaxing and enjoyable and Michael did not allow her to do anything; telling her that she needed to rest. They watched movies and roasted marshmallows over the fire.

They were lying right in front of the fireplace where he had spread a thick throw rug on the beautiful board floor. The cabin was too large to be a cabin and she had told him so the minute she saw it. It was more like a log mansion.

He had firmly told her before they left the house that there would be no talk of work or anything concerning work and she had told him of course not. His mother had left for her cruise early that morning and would not be back until the following week Friday.

"My dad and I used to come here most times and we would fish and swim in the lake out back. We were men so we would get away from the frills and eat what we killed." He told her with a whimsical smile.

She turned her head to look up at him and he looked down at her. "Mom was right," he commented softly. "You have made such a difference in our lives that I don't know what I did before you." He had on the watch she had given him and had told her huskily that he would never take it off again.

"Remember those relationships I told you about?" she asked him. He nodded. "I thought I would never be involved in another one because it was too painful and then I tried to fill the void with my job and it worked for a while," she smiled absently. "That was until you came into my life and I realized there was so much more to life. You gave me so much

Michael, I don't know how to begin to tell you how much I appreciate it."

"I should be thanking you baby," he told her lovingly. "I played the field for so many years because I was restless and looking for you, now this is it for me my love; I don't see anyone else but you."

With a gentle smile Andrea pulled his head down to hers and showed him how much his words affected her.

Later that night they slept in each other's arms and in the morning they bundled up and went outside to see the snowflakes coming down. They had a white Christmas after all.

Chapter 10

The months flew by rapidly with work and preparation for the baby. The nursery had been decorated with Gloria constantly changing or adding something. Andrea had jokingly told her that they were going to have a hard time getting the baby out of the nursery because of the way it looked.

The month of April stepped in with the cold lingering but not unpleasantly so and Andrea who had been at home for the past month was starting to go stir crazy. The doctor had told her that she was due to deliver by the middle of the month and she could not wait. Her extended stomach was making her feel weary and restless. Michael had been doing his best to be with her as often as possible but with work and meetings and the trips he had put off, he was very busy and he kept apologizing to her.

She had to admit she was feeling a little resentful that she was stuck at the house and he got to go to work; she was not made to be idle. Millie had been by to see her several times and kept her up to date on office gossip. Her assistant had gotten involved with Jerome from accounts and there was a budding office romance going on.

She still did some work from home but if she allowed her husband he would not let her lift a finger. Gloria was not much better, letting Bertie cook whatever she wanted and taking it to her wherever she was.

She looked at the calendar for the umpteenth time as if by looking at it she could fast forward the date. She got up slowly, rubbing a hand against her back. It was the twentieth of April and still the baby had not made his arrival. She had asked the doctor if there was some way she could convince the baby that it was time to get out of her womb and the doctor had laughed. “Little Michael will come when he is good and ready, my dear Andrea.”

She stared at her reflection in the full length mirror; she had gotten so big that she could not believe it was her body. Michael was constantly telling her that she was perfect.

Gloria bustled inside the room after knocking on the door of the living room. It was almost twelve o’clock and she was making sure Andrea had something to eat. Michael had wanted to hire a full time helper for her but she had said no; she was at loose ends now so what little there was to do she would do it. He had warned her that if he found out that she was doing any heavy lifting or cleaning, he was going to go over her and hire someone. She had made a face at him and not commented.

“Bertie made grilled cheese sandwich and there’s milk and cookies and a salad,” Gloria set the tray on the table beside the couch and glanced at her daughter in law in concern. She looked tired, she thought sympathetically, it was getting near to the time so it was getting hard for her to move around. Michael felt he should be near her but she had insisted that he went to the office; they would call if anything.

Gloria had been in the nursery for a little while making sure everything was okay and ready for when the baby came.

“Thanks Gloria,” Andrea put aside the baby book she had been reading.

“Your husband said I should check on you because you ordered him off the phone a while ago.” Gloria told her teasingly.

“My husband and your son is driving me crazy,” Andrea retorted. “He has been calling me every five or so minutes so I told him if he called again I am not going to answer the phone." She bit into the sandwich with relish. Bertie made the best grilled cheese sandwich she had ever tasted.

"That's why he has resorted to calling me and harassing me," Gloria said with a laugh. "How are you dear?"

"I am okay just a bit tired and impatient to get this child out of me," she rubbed her hand over her swollen belly with a whimsical smile. "I just want to see him."

"I know how you feel," Gloria told her, taking a seat next to her. "When I was pregnant with your husband, I drove Michael crazy telling him we needed to go to the doctor because the baby was taking too long to come. I woke him up all hours of the night saying that something was wrong. I was a neurotic mess and I am sure he was secretly glad we were not able to have another child." Gloria laughed gently. "My poor husband put up with my nonsense and never complained; bless his soul and on top of that he had a company to run."

"Now he is the one driving me crazy," Andrea said with a rueful laugh.

She finished eating and they went to the nursery to look at and admire the finished look. It was wall papered with all sorts of animals and the paper was a soft pastel blue. There was a lovely mural on one side of the wall depicting a bubbling brook and several deer drinking from it. The crib was a strong oak with a beautiful hand crafted mobile suspended over it that played different types of classical music. Gloria had put in a comfortable rocking chair with a soft cushion for when she was feeding the baby and there was the changing table, a beautiful dresser and a bassinet that Michael had had shipped from London. Andrea had left Michael sleeping some nights just to come in and sit in the rocker and talked to her baby in the quietness of the early morning when she found it hard to sleep. Michael had woken up a few times and discovered she was not beside him and had come to find her and stayed. They had fallen asleep several nights there with her in his lap.

He came home early that evening as she and Gloria were in the living room watching television. Her heart always quickened its beat every time she saw him; he was so handsome that she fell in love with him all over again.

“Hi mom,” he kissed his mother’s cheek softly before turning to his wife and pulling her up against him, he kissed her passionately on the lips, leaving Andrea leaning weakly against him. "How was work?" she asked him when she got her breath back.

"Very good," he went on to tell her what had transpired at the office. "How was your day? And after you banned me from calling you, I had to call Mom to find out if you were doing all right." He told her reprovingly.

She laughed at him, her arms wrapped around his neck. "You were driving me crazy Michael. How on earth do you get any work done if you call me so often?"

"That's the advantage of being the boss," he kissed her again on the lips and they went upstairs together as was the practice. She would stay with him while he took a shower and they would talk about the day and then they would come back downstairs to have supper. Gloria had gone into the kitchen to consult with Bertie about the menu. Even though Michael and Andrea had their own kitchen they always had dinner with Gloria much to the delight of the older woman.

After dinner, they stayed downstairs for a while chatting until Michael saw that Andrea was starting to get sleepy and they retired upstairs. He made love to her gently and lovingly and afterwards he sponged down her body because she was feeling a little uncomfortable. His hands lingered on her belly feeling the restless movements of his child inside her. It always humbled him to know that his seed had grown inside her and she was carrying his baby – it made him want to go to the moon and beyond for her; this woman whom he loved so unconditionally.

“He wants to come into the world, to see his mommy and daddy,” he said softly as he rubbed the special cream on her to prevent stretch marks.

“And I want him to come out and stop using my body as a football,” Andrea told him with a smile as his hands lingered on her belly.

“I love you so much baby and I am so scared,” Michael admitted, staring at her; his green eyes cloudy with fear. “I don’t want anything to happen to you, both of you.”

“Nothing will,” Andrea told him softly, placing her hand against his. “We have to think positive darling, very soon we will have little Michael crying at all hours and keeping us up at night.”

“Are we really going to call him little Michael?” her husband asked with a rueful smile.

“We can always call him Mickey or his middle name: Andre or L.M. instead of little Michael.” Andrea suggested.

He wrinkled his brow in concentration. “Maybe,” he said uncertainly, bending down to kiss her belly. He stood and reached behind her to place another pillow under her head before turning out the lights and climbing in beside her.

*****

The pains started at four a.m. At first, just little twinges that had her gasping and when it reached some minutes to five she started feeling the sharp piercing jabs as if someone was poking her belly with a hot iron. Her scream woke him up in terror and he jumped out of the bed and turned on the light to see her face bathed in sweat and tight with pain. His heart slammed inside his chest and he reached for the phone to call first the doctor and then his mother.

“Breathe baby,” he told her, trying not to panic. Gloria was there in a few minutes and with a calm that said she had been there before she took over from her terrified son. The doctor told them to get her ready and he would meet them at the hospital.

They were on their way to the hospital in minutes with Michael driving and Gloria in the back seat with her. Michael broke every traffic rule in his haste to get her there and his mother had to tell him that he would be defeating the purpose if he got them killed. Andrea was trying hard not to cry out as the pain came upon her but to breathe as she had been taught to do in Lamaze class.

When they got to the hospital, the doctor was outside waiting for them with a stretcher and she was wheeled immediately in the emergency room. She was five centimeters dilated and the doctor told them that the baby was making his way out.

Michael put on the surgical garb and Gloria was in the waiting area. Andrea was given something to help with the pain so it was not so bad but her husband sat beside her anxiously holding her hand as the doctor instructed her when to push.

"You're doing very well Andrea," he said kindly. "I can see him crowning now. Just give one little push and then hold on for a little bit."

Michael had her head propped up against his chest and he could feel the pain vibrating through her body. "It's okay baby," he whispered, wiping the sweat off her brow and just wanted her to stop feeling so much pain; it was killing him to see her like this.

"One more push Andrea," the doctor told her. Andrea did as she was told and gripping her husband's hand. She gave a strong push, sagging back against Michael and smiling wearily as she heard her son's lusty cry.

"He has strong vocals," the doctor said with a smile as the nurse took him and wrapped him into a blanket; taking him to meet his parents.

Both Andrea and Michael looked at the red screwed up face of their son as he made his presence known. "Look baby, our son," Michael said in awe as Andrea took him into her arms in wonder, his little hands moving all over the place.

"He's perfect," she whispered, holding on to his little fingers. She was very tired as if she had run a marathon but she felt as if she could hold him forever. "No woman is ever going to be good enough for you." She told him, laying her cheek against his curly black hair.

They took him away to wash him off and cleaned her up. When they brought him back all cleaned up and dressed in a tiny onesie; Gloria had come into the room and the three of them kept staring at him until the nurse came and told them that both mother and baby needed their rest.

Michael stayed with her while she slept and when she woke up she felt as if she could eat a whole restaurant of food; she was starving.

Her husband was still lying beside her fast asleep and Andrea reached out to push back the black curls from his strong forehead. Little Michael looked so much like him; minus the green eyes, his eyes were golden brown but she knew that the color of his eyes would probably change.

“Hey you,” he murmured opening his eyes to look up at her. “How is my son’s mother?”

“Starving,” she admitted ruefully. “I could eat everything in sight; your son has left a vacuum inside me.”

“I will get you something to eat right away,” he pulled out his phone and ordered food from their favorite restaurant.

“Michael, you know I could get something from the hospital,” she protested.

“Only the best is good enough for my wife and the mother of my son.” He told her giving her a kiss. “And speaking of which, this is for you.” He pulled out a small red velvet box from his pocket.

“Michael what have you done?” she stared at the box. “I have more jewelry than I can ever wear,” she took the box and opened it expecting something extravagant only to find an exquisite topaz ring with emerald stones all around it; and engraved inside was : ‘To my darling wife on the delivery of our son.’ Love your husband Michael.’

He slid the ring onto her right ring finger and Andrea stared at the lights flashing off it. “It’s beautiful,” she told him huskily as he pulled her into his arms.

“Thank you,” he whispered above her head. “For being my wife and carrying my child.”

“You’re welcome;” she whispered softly.

The restaurant came with so many different dishes that Andrea had to give some to people in the rooms near to hers. She fed her son and they went back to sleep. When she woke up next her room was filled with flowers and balloons and gift baskets from the office. Gloria had gone home to get some sleep but would be back later. Michael refused to leave and when Andrea woke up she saw him holding their son and talking to him quietly. She gazed at the picture they made and felt the tears coming to her eyes. It was the most beautiful picture she had ever seen. The two men in her life.

He looked up and saw her staring at them and smiled. “Hi Mrs. Wade, we were just wondering when you would wake up.”

“I have to be the most fortunate woman in the entire world,” she told him, reaching out her arms for her son as he brought him over. Little Michael transferred his gaze from his father to her and she kissed his soft baby cheeks.

“Millie said she is coming over, I told her she could.” He told her, brushing back the wisp of hair on her forehead. It was a Thursday and he had no intention of leaving his wife and child and going into the office.

Andrea nodded, her eyes still on her baby. “He’s so beautiful,” she murmured, looking at his little features.

"So is his mom," Michael told her. She looked up and caught the look of intense love on his face and her heart started beating rapidly.

"I love you Michael," she whispered as he bent his head and kissed her tenderly on the lips. That was how Millie found them and she thought about stepping back from the tender moment but Michael raised his head and saw her at the door.

"Come on in Millie, I was just about to get some coffee," he told her, giving her hand a quick squeeze before leaving.

Millie put the huge basket she had been carrying with the rest. "You're going to need a truck to carry all these things home." She told her friend dryly; coming over to gaze at the little boy who was quietly suckling at his mother's breast.

"I am planning to leave it for the patients in the cancer unit," Andrea told her friend, raising her cheek for her kiss.

"You are a mother, welcome to the club," Millie teased. "He's so perfect and looks so much like his father what a surprise."

"I can't believe how much I love him already Millie; I don't want to let him go." Andrea said in wonder as she transferred him to her other breast. “Now I see what Michael had been saying to me all along; I don’t know when I will be back at work.”

Millie laughed and she started telling her friend what had been happening in her absence. They sat there admiring Little Michael until the nurse came to get him for his rest.

*****

Andrea and her son went home Sunday afternoon after the doctor had made sure that both mother and son were in good health. Michael guided her inside and straight into the nursery where there was a huge welcome home ‘Little Michael Andre Wade’ was put up in his nursery. Gloria, with the help of the helper, had unpacked his clothes and made sure everything was within reach.

Andrea sat in the rocker and Michael elevated her feet on the hammock and made sure his wife and son were comfortable. Gloria came and took him from her so that she could get some sleep. It was a little past five o’clock but Andrea realized she was feeling tired and the doctor had told her to get as much rest as she could.

She woke up at dusk to find her husband moving silently around the room. “Michael?” she said drowsily.

“Oh baby sorry, I was trying hard not to wake you,” he said contritely coming over to the bed. The glaring red light on the clock said it was already eight o’clock. “Little Michael is sleeping; I just checked on him.” He told her before she could ask.

“Are you hungry?” he propped her up on the pillow and brushed the hair from her face.

“Starving,” she admitted with a laugh. “But could you call and ask someone to bring something up? I want you to stay with me.”

“Sure my love,” he came and laid beside her on the bed; reaching for the phone and calling down to the kitchen to talk to Bertie.

Their food was brought up within minutes and they ate, putting the tray aside. Andrea rested her head on his shoulder and placed her hand inside his shirt to feel his warm chest; sighing in contentment. “I am glad I am home,” she murmured. “The hospital was great but I feel more comfortable at home.”

“I am glad you’re home too,” her husband said softly. “I am not sure we should have another child,” he told her suddenly, one hand running down her back.

She raised her head to look at him. “Why not?”

“I had to see you in so much pain and could not do anything about it,” he shook his head as he remembered how he felt when she had screamed out after experiencing the first contraction. He had wanted to die.

“It’s over and done with Michael and women were made for childbearing.” Andrea told him gently, smoothing out the tenseness on his face. “I love you and our son. Maybe I will want another child but it’s something we will discuss later on.”

“You’re amazing, do you know that?” he asked her huskily, kissing her pert little nose.

“And you’re a wonderful husband and you’re going to be a terrific father.” She said.

They clung to each other for a little while then went to the nursery together to stare at their sleeping son, his tiny little fists bunched up against his cheek as he slept peacefully.

Michael closed his hands around his wife and they stood there looking at their son; and his smile burst forth. He had his family and nothing else mattered at all.

The end.

If you enjoyed this ebook and want me to keep writing more, please leave a review of it on the store where you bought it. By doing so you'll allow me more time to write these books for you as they'll get more exposure. So thank you. :)

Get Free Romance eBooks!

Hi there. As a special thank you for buying this book, for a limited time I want to send you some great ebooks completely **free of charge** directly to your email! You can get it by going to this page:

www.saucyromancebooks.com/physical

You can see a the cover of these books on the next page:

www.AfroRomanceBooks.com/RomanceBooks

These ebooks are so exclusive you can't even buy them. When you download them I'll also send you updates when new books like this are available.

Again, that link is:

www.saucyromancebooks.com/physical

Now, if you enjoyed the book you just read, please leave a positive review of it where you bought it (e.g. Amazon). It'll help get it out there a lot more and mean I can continue writing these books for you. So thank you. :)

More Books By Shani Badu

If you enjoyed that, you'll love Steven And Julie by J A Fielding (search 'Steven And Julie by J A Fielding' on Amazon to get it now).

Also available: My Kind Of Bad by Erica A Davis (search 'My Kind Of Bad Erica A Davis' on Amazon to get it now).

You can also get more sexy books by BWWM Club by searching for them on Amazon.

You can also see other related books by myself and other top romance authors at:

www.saucyromancebooks.com/romancebooks

Made in the USA
Lexington, KY
25 April 2018